MW00720095

Don't Admit You're in Assisted Living
Mystery # 2 The Wet Bathing Suit

By

Dorothy Seymour Mills

Love to the Mills Family

from nancy

The contents of this book regarding the accuracy of events, people and places depicted; permissions to use all previously published materials; all are the sole responsibility of the author, who assumes all liability for the contents of this book.

© 2017 Dorothy Seymour Mills

eBook ISBN 13: 978-1-60452-134-4
Softcover ISBN 13: 978-1-60452-131-3
Hardcover ISBN 13: 978-1-60452-137-5
Library of Congress Control Number: 2017958423

BluewaterPress LLC
52 Tuscan Way Ste 202-309
Saint Augustine FL 32092

http://bluewaterpress.com

Please note that address information is subject to change. At the time of printing, the address was correct, but may have changed since. Please check our website for the latest address information for BluewaterPress LLC.

Foreword

The idea of reaching an advanced age and moving into an apartment building full of others just as old or older may sound uninviting. You may even shrink from it, or call out "No way! I'm never going to get that old."

But communities set up entirely for seniors are so attractive and offer so much that they've been magnets for the elderly, who fill them as soon as they are built.

More than 735,000 people now live in assisted living in the United States. Florida in particular has become a place where living facilities designed especially for seniors have proliferated. In Florida alone, 73,000 residents occupy the assisted living communities of the state.

More than half the residents of these communities have reached the age of 85 or older. In fact, the typical assisted living resident is an 87-year-old female who needs help with two or three activities of daily living (like showering or dressing) and has two or three of the top ten chronic conditions (like COPD, stroke, heart disease, or diabetes).

In other words, these are people (mostly women) who are past being active physically and whose ability to contribute to modern life is limited by physical decline and encroaching age-connected illness.

However, these people still desire to take part in activities in which they can succeed, and they haven't stopped thinking. Moreover, they would like to have some fun, and they can even laugh at themselves.

Why would anyone want to live in one of these senior communities? What is it like to live there?

Well, it's different. I have lived in one for years, and I find that it's the right place for me at this time in my life.

In the community where I live, I can have as much privacy and as much social life as I wish. And I can get as much help as I need.

Reading about the fictional Locksley Glen I have created for this book may give you an idea of what you could experience if you should decide to live in one of these facilities. You might find out that you agree with me.

I must warn you that this is a place where sometimes everything seems completely normal, and the people are like the ones you've known under other circumstances. Other times, things get a little crazy. But as you will notice, living in such a place can be entertaining—and sometimes downright hilarious.

Of course, I may have exaggerated everything just a little!

To write this book, I have borrowed a few events, words, and people (or parts thereof) from persons I've met, especially those who reside with me at The Carlisle in Naples, Florida. I hope they don't mind, and I thank them for persuading me to write this book.

Dorothy Seymour Mills
July 5, 2016, which is my 88th birthday

Second Mystery: The Wet Bathing Suit

O N E

L ooking back at it, I can understand how our obsession seems a little weird.

I mean our fixation on finding out who had left a soggy bathing suit at the pool court and never claimed it. Why would the ownership of a discarded article of clothing become a mystery we felt we had to solve? Probably because we have so little to concern us besides our health.

At Locksley Glen, the senior community we live in, we don't have to think about cooking, cleaning, laundry, or home upkeep and repairs. Those matters are taken care of for us. So our minds become fixed on an anomaly like the Wet Bathing Suit.

I realize now that our curiosity grew partly because we visualize someone taking it off and walking away without a stitch on. There's no changing room in the pool court, so taking off one's bathing suit would be done in full view of anyone who looked out the window of an apartment that faced the court.

The sexiness of this thought is undeniable. But then, the lush beauty of the pool court is a sexy kind of beauty.

Nothing attracts prospective residents to Locksley Glen more than its pool, situated in an atrium inside a ring of apartments and landscaped with a variety of tropical trees, bushes, and flowering plants. The court area includes small pools surrounded with rocks penetrated by tiny waterfalls. People being shown Locksley Glen's assets stop walking and stare with wonder through the glass doors that open into the pool court. They're mesmerized by the striking blue-and-white tiled pool and its tropical surroundings. I've heard exclamations like "Wow! A movie-star pool!"

Residents of Locksley Glen admire the pool court, too. That doesn't mean they actually use the pool, however. The pool is short, about ten strokes the long way, and quite shallow, with water at the deep end reaching only to my chin (and I'm five feet six). Serious swimmers find it limiting. Besides, water ruins hairdos. And today's skimpy bathing suits expose our aging bodies cruelly.

But as a place to lounge, nothing can beat the pool court. The gentle wind stirs the palms softly and circulates the scent of the gorgeous flowers to the noses of people who retreat to this patio just to sit, read, chat, doze, stare at the scenery — and who knows what else? They also come to pollute the air with cigarette smoke. Smoking is not allowed, but it happens anyway.

So when an unidentified wet two-piece bathing suit was discovered lying on a chaise longue, residents were intrigued. Requests for the owner to come forward and identify her swimsuit came to nothing.

Those few people known to actually swim in the pool, or at least paddle around in it, swore that the suit did not belong to them. A visitor could not have left it because it was discovered two weeks after Easter/Passover, a period when no resident had relatives visiting at Locksley Glen.

So who dropped a wet bathing suit there, in full view of the surrounding apartments, and left the area wearing, at the most, only the required bathing suit cover? We all knew how skimpy those garments are. Some are made of see-through material. To imagine a resident appearing in the halls wearing only this abbreviated and revealing costume shocked us. Or at least we let people think we were shocked.

Actually, we were titillated.

Some residents hastened to explain why they could not be the owner of that two-piece black model. Katrina declared during Happy Hour, "I own just one bathing suit, a blue and white one, which matches the colors of the pool tiles. Never would I appear in that two-piece black jobbie anyway." With her hair in a crown of braids, Katrina seemed like an angelic Goody Two-Shoes, Maybe she protested too much. Could Katrina be the real culprit?

Probably not.

Starr, after a few sips of a martini, admitted, "I have never set foot in the pool and would never do so because my coiffure is too expensive to ruin." She touched her black bangs possessively. "Besides," she added, "chlorine in the water is bad for the skin." Would a vain woman like Starr, an ex-travel agent with self-conscious elegance, strip down to the buff in our pool court, surrounded as it was by the windows and lanais of residents' apartments?

Maybe....Oh, I guess not.

Barbie Boobs had a good alibi, too. "I stay away from the pool area because I'm allergic to the sun. Besides, I hate sun hats. They mash down one's hairdo." And she tossed her curly yellow locks, kept curly and yellow by assiduous visits to the Locksley Glen hairdresser.

We had no reason to doubt Barbie.

There are other reasons for staying away from the pool. Nobody mentioned the picturesque but bumpy brick pathways through the pool area that make walking difficult for people our age. Residents without confidence in their balance seldom venture into the area. We hate to admit it, but we lack the sure-footed equanimity of the young.

When I entered the Dining Room to have dinner with Joan and her husband Clarence, along with Ed Champion, our jovial Kentuckian, and Helene, master of the acerbic remark, Joan started to talk about the bathing suit mystery even before the soup arrived.

"Well, Alice One, have you discovered whose bathing suit was left at the pool?"

"No," I responded with surprise. "Did you expect me to have the answer?"

"We all did," Clarence replied for her. "I'm sure you were the one who powered the investigation into the Petros problem."

"Where is Petros, by the way?"

"Working as a waiter at my favorite Naples restaurant, the Club Manhattan on Fifth Avenue," Clarence told us, smiling with satisfaction.

"Unsurprising," said Helene. "You had nothing to do with his obtaining this plum position, of course," she remarked with her usual irony.

"Of course," Clarence replied. "But it took a bit of persuasion."

"Involving… bribery?" Helene was persistent.

Clarence searched his mind for the appropriate reply, then came up with "Huge kickbacks from the waiter."

When we had all finished laughing, Helene reopened the question of the week. "I, too, have a good excuse for not swimming, although I enjoyed the Tuesday pool exercises led by Marjorie Metabolis, the instructor from the Y, despite her regrettably authoritarian manner. I'm not visiting the pool these days because I'm unable to re-enter the water until the sore on my bum knee has healed."

"How is that sore, Helene?" asked Joan. "And is it the result of your last fall?"

"Slow to heal, and, yes, because of a fall. But the sore doesn't bother me as much as being unable to have a drink before dinner because of continually taking drugs to help it heal. Evidently, alcohol and drugs refuse to get along. Fruit juice is extremely boring without rum."

"That will pass," said Ed Champion. He began to insert some of his Kentucky drawl. "Meanwhile, we men are all tantalahzed by imaginin' one of you emergin' from the pool withaout her suit and not botherin' to take it home. Who the heck does it belong to?"

"Actually," said Clarence, "it's mine."

"Your body type would do nothing for the top of that suit, Clarence."

"I stuffed those pockets with dead palm fronds."

For the second time, Clarence made us laugh, conjuring in our minds the picture of this small man standing in front of the pool in a woman's two-piece black bathing suit with brown palm fronds sticking out of the bra section. My mind went on to imagine the rest of the scenario, with Katrina nearby looking at him in surprise while wearing a tiny, wet blue-and-white facsimile of her Dutch traditional dress, Clarence's wife Joan in her usual shocking-pink one-piecer walking toward him determined to push him into the pool as punishment for such demeaning behavior, while Helene, a huge white bandage on her knee, called to Marge Metabolis for help in rescuing Clarence...

"Alice One," I heard Joan calling. "You're in one of your reveries, aren't you? Stop imagining ridiculous scenes. The salads have been served."

Just then Heather Hamm, a small, round woman, walked by our table. She bore a vague look on her face. Her blouse hung limply outside her rumpled skirt. Her walk seemed aimless rather than purposeful. She looked about her as though unsure of her destination.

Heather was followed in a few moments by Thalia St. Clair, the Dining Room hostess, calling, "Mrs. Hamm, Mrs. Hamm! This way, please, let me seat you, Mrs. Hamm...."

Heather finally became aware of Thalia and responded to her calls. Her pause permitted the hostess, who was clad in her usual long, swishy skirt, to guide her in the other direction to a table with an empty seat. We looked at each other meaningfully.

"Uh-oh," said Katrina. "It looks as though Heather is losing it." Katrina has a habit of pointing out the obvious, as everyone may know by now.

None of us added any remarks until Helene thought of one. "Maybe it was Heather who lost her bathing suit."

Joan shook her head slowly. "Never. She's got to be at least a size 14," said the woman who may have reached size six.

"Whoa," said Katrina, putting down her soup spoon. "Maybe we have the wrong idea about the meaning of that discarded suit. Perhaps the removal of the suit was not voluntary." We looked at her in surprise. "Perhaps what we are looking at is a clue to a crime. Think about it: do women normally remove their bathing suits poolside?"

"Oh, come on, Katrina," said Ed. "You think we have a monster here, a sex fiend?" He shook his head. "I've seen no evidence that such a person lives at Locksley Glen." He finished his coffee with a flourish.

"Never heard any questionable conversation from a man here?" Katrina pursued.

"Never," he asserted. "You, Clarence?"

His mouth full of salad, the man in question shook his head.

"Let's forget about that as a possible explanation," Joan proposed. But we didn't forget.

TWO

At breakfast the next morning we were full of comments about the activities director's list of upcoming excursions because he had included something called Bone Valley. At first we found nobody who admitted to having visited the place.

"A couple of years ago I visited the Collier County Museum, which is number three on the list," said Katrina, "but I can't imagine being interested in going somewhere to see bones. Why would we want to do that?"

Then Lucas revealed that once long ago he had visited Bone Valley briefly and learned that the bones discovered there were said to be those of prehistoric animals, found in an area where the soil happened to contain preservative elements.

"What animals?" asked Joyce Joslin. "I don't like dogs."

"The usual saber-toothed tiger, mastodon, giant sloth...."

"Ugh. Sounds unattractive," Annabelle contributed.

"I like the idea," said Barbie Boobs. "I always thought digging up the past would be interesting."

I joined her by nodding and saying, "I think I'll go on that trip. Who knows? It may inspire some painting ideas."

That's all I heard for a while about Bone Valley, a place that was to loom larger in our consciousness.

The next topic that arose at my table was the new film, *Walk Away*, featuring the heartthrob actor Chris Markel, whose blond hair became blonder with each new film.

It was Annabelle who changed the subject and brought up Markel's new movie. "I watched that Chris Markel film last night — for a while, until I couldn't stand the language any longer."

Joyce Joslin added, "I know. We don't need to hear that kind of talk. I switched to *Current Crime Diary* so that I didn't have to listen to that vulgar word in every sentence. Barbie, you're facing the right way. Can you catch the eye of the coffee server?"

"Yes, but *Current Crime Diary* has a shootout in nearly every scene," replied Barbie, "with a lot of characters falling over and bleeding heavily. By the end of the show," she continued, "practically everybody is dead, just like an opera. Who wants to watch all that death? We have enough of it here."

Joyce Joslin exclaimed, "Ooh! I just dropped a blueberry on my yellow pedal pushers." She loved wearing pants named for an activity she hadn't engaged in for fifty years.

Lucas, reaching for the butter, assured her, "Don't worry, none of us still have vision good enough to notice a blueberry stain, even if it's on yellow pants.

"As for *Walk Away*, I stuck with it until that sex scene in which he tears the bathing suit off a reluctant Suzy Plankton. Then I... walked away. I didn't need that much detail to get the message that Markel's character is savagely coercive. Today's movies overdo that stuff."

"I agree," said Bob Avery. "Movie directors leave nothing to the imagination. Anyone locate the pepper?"

By then, Katrina and I were looking at each other, both of us thinking about Lucas's reminder of a scene in the Chris Markel film. It was Joan, however, who spoke out. "Some of us are beginning to worry about the possibility that the wet bathing suit at the pool might have been forcibly removed. Now, with the example of the Chris Markel movie, we're getting nervous. Does anyone think the discarded suit signals foul play?"

Heads went up from plates.

"Good heavens!" Annabelle exclaimed.

"Joan, you take movies too seriously," said her husband Clarence.

"But if the suit is the sign of an attack, then the woman involved might be reluctant to say anything about it. Maybe that's why nobody has come forward to claim it."

We thought about this possibility. Could this be the reason that the owner of the suit hadn't identified herself?

Clarence shook his head. It was he who used the word in the forefront of our minds but were hesitant to speak. "I don't think we're dealing with a rapist. Consider the people you've met here. Nobody has ever shown one sign of cruelty."

Joyce demurred. "Bad things do happen," she said. "Think back through your life. We've all experienced something, or our families or friends have, that's unexpectedly evil." She dipped her napkin into her glass of water and began scrubbing at the blueberry stain.

"I haven't," insisted Barbie. "I believe that everyone is inherently good."

"I think it's too easy to get carried away," Lucas opined. "I'm sure the suit is a clue to nothing more than carelessness."

"I have another question," Annabelle volunteered. "Where is the brother of our former server Petros? The one who changed his name from Stavros to Steve and worked at our front desk for a while." We all relaxed a bit. The change in topic away from a topic that was too serious to think about for long lifted the tension.

"Bill Hufferman told me that Clarence helped Stavros get into the CCC. Not the government youth organization of the

1930s" (that drew a chuckle) "but Collier County College," Bob responded.

"Good," Annabelle said. "Stavros is launched on his life. Working here would eventually become a dead end."

"Not really," declared Bob. "Did you know that President Obama was once a waiter in an assisted living facility?"

"You're kidding."

"No, it's true. He said it was a neat job. His only problem was that sometimes the residents were cranky because of being on restricted diets: they might want more salt even if they weren't allowed to have it."

"Cranky? Who wouldn't be cranky? Getting old is not for wimps," Joyce put in.

"Have you seen the new ads listing ways for combating FOGO?" asked Barbie, her bright eyes sparkling with humor.

"What the heck is FOGO? Is it related to Old Fogies?"

"It's an acronym. The letters stand for 'Fear Of Getting Old.'"

"What's the point of fearing something that's inevitable?" Bob was waving at a passing server. "More coffee, please, Anton. So what are the ads about?"

"Just a pharmaceutical company urging us to think old age can be the best time of our lives."

Annabelle laughed. "Preposterous. With all these things happening to our bodies? The older we get, the richer those pharmaceutical companies become from all the pills we take to combat the effects of aging. I don't mind admitting that right now I'm taking eleven different pills. My life is an open bush."

We all looked up at her. Open bush?

She went on relentlessly. "Our old age may be the best time of the drug companies' lives, but not ours."

"That's a negative attitude if I ever heard one," Bob Avery responded. "I think it's true that the less fear we have about aging, the more we'll enjoy it. I, for one, intend to enjoy it as much as I can. Did you read what Maya Angelou said recently about aging? She said, 'The eighties are hot! You want to try to make it there if you can.'" And Bob took another bite of cinnamon coffee cake.

I thought: Bob is certainly recovering from having lost his friend and constant companion, Mary One, to death just last year. At least he's not permanently feeling sorry for himself and refusing to get out of bed, the way a resident named Ronald Price did a couple of years ago, when he lost his spouse. What did that get Ronald? A stroke.

But I kept these thoughts to myself.

Lucas weighed in with what sounded like an aphorism: "Aging is... adulthood... adulterated by illness."

We accepted this apt evaluation without comment.

Bob returned to our original concern. "I still wonder whose bathing suit that is. It's rather shapely. It would fit someone with a good figure." And he looked around the table at the women in view.

Annabelle and I raised our eyebrows at this remark. "You like seeing scanty two-piece bathing suits on women?" I posed to him with a smile.

"Sure." Then he added, "My life is an open bush, too." We saw a sly grin when he repeated Annabelle's unusual phrase. Then he went on. "Two-piece bathing suits remind me of what the humorist Dorothy Parker once wrote in the *New Yorker* magazine: 'Brevity is the soul of... lingerie.'"

"Bob," said Annabelle, "you certainly don't suffer from the new disease of FOGO." Then she called for her walker. Finally, she announced, "I'm off to practice for the Locksley Glen Olympics."

"Doing what?" asked Lucas.

"Poker. Texas Cold 'em."

"You mean Hold 'em."

"That's what I said. We play in that cold room named the Big Game Room." And, pulling on a sweater, she departed, pushing her walker.

"Did you ever get the idea that Annabelle has trouble hearing?"

Lucas responded. "Just trouble finding her hearing aids each morning. She lives in the apartment next to mine. We leave at about the same time. If she's misplaced her hearing aids, she doesn't hear me slam my door, so she doesn't know I'm there—until I poke her on the shoulder, and that makes her jump." Lucas chuckled, as if startling Annabelle was a gratifying activity.

We old people get gratification from small things.

Just then Handsome Harry came by, herding a group of prospective residents and explaining to them the amenities they could expect if they lived at Locksley Glen.

Harry Tremaine is the Glen's rental agent. He can rattle off the advantages of living here without making his spiel seem mechanical. Handsome Harry, as we call him, makes the ideal salesman, except for being youthful and therefore looking out of place here.

Harry's enthusiasm for living at Locksley Glen is sometimes hard to accept. What would such a young man know about giving up some of your independence in exchange for getting the help you need?

For example, how could he ever know what it feels like to have your son or daughter confiscate the keys to your car because your eyesight is bad and your reaction time has dropped into the danger zone? How could he understand the way our age-related bodily limitations make us grouchy because we don't want to accept them? The answer is that he couldn't.

But his job is to present the favorable aspects of living in an institution like Locksley Glen, and his performances have helped a lot of people find a comfortable life here.

We heard Harry describe our Dining Room as "open continuously for twelve hours a day and the venue for fine dining." True. The dining room is open from seven A.M. to seven P.M. and serves delicious food in generous amounts, although the menu doesn't vary enough for some of us, and the pickings for vegetarians and vegans remain meager.

But we manage nicely by supplementing our Glen meals with occasional ventures to the downtown restaurants for lunch or dinner, despite their exorbitant prices. A few of us still do part of our own cooking and baking—that is, when our arthritis permits.

Too often, this common ailment prevents us from engaging in activities we have always loved, like baking chocolate chip cookies, but it has an up side because it also relieves us from having to perform things we have always hated, like laundering, ironing, and cleaning.

"Now, ladies and gentlemen," we heard Harry say, "I'm going to show you our lovely pool. This way."

Right again. The pool is lovely.

Hearing Harry give some of his spiel made me remember his favorite story, which he tells often to residents: "One day I was squiring around the Glen a couple of frail old people in their nineties with their granddaughter, who was trying to convince them to move into an apartment here, where she wouldn't have to worry about them and they could get the assistance they needed. The white-haired man—who limped, was very much bent forwards, and leaned heavily on a cane—was resisting the move. His granddaughter asked why he wouldn't consider it, and he replied 'Living here is for old folks.'"

It's true that we have difficulty considering ourselves as old. As several of us left the Dining Room, I realized all over again that I was old and tired, too, but I blamed the feeling on having worked late the evening before on a still life I had started painting.

Breakfast didn't revive me the way it often does, so I decided to go to the pool court and have a swim. I made a mental note to ask my doctor if I qualified for a series of

Vitamin B shots. Of course, mental notes rarely work, but occasionally I recall their content for a day or two.

At my apartment I rummaged in my bathing suit drawer, where I keep an assortment of suits, and picked out a dark green one. I put on my white beach coat (it just covers my knees, which have unaccountably become bony) and matching strappy slippers. Finally, I pinned up my hair so that it wouldn't drag in the water and left for the pool.

I'm vain about my beige hair. It's always been beige — with the help of various colorists over the years.

Just entering the open-air pool area makes me feel relaxed. The warm tropical breeze causes me to half-close my eyes and imagine I am vacationing on an island in the Pacific where a brown woman in a flowered sarong sings "Bali Hai" and a small, obsequious servant brings me a tall, cold raspberry-colored rum drink with an orange slice perched on the edge.

I know I have an overly-vivid imagination, one that causes me to constantly imagine alternative scenarios, but I enjoy having it. It's mine, and I'm not giving it up.

Sighing in relief, I threw off my beach coat and slippers and, taking firm hold of the banister, walked down the broad steps into the pool... and suddenly realized someone was there, at the other end of the pool. My weakening eyesight occasionally causes me to overlook someone in the distance.

Like six feet away.

He called out "Hello!" and I realized it must be a New Man.

His bald head shone in the sun. On the top of his head perched a Band-Aid, where his dermatologist must have removed a growth caused by sun damage. It's something we've all gotten used to seeing.

Dermatologists loom large in the lives of people our age because when we were growing up, nobody had access to skin lotions that protected us from harmful rays. As a result, we have all suffered the removal of unwanted, and sometimes dangerous, skin growths. Both men and women appear in the common rooms wearing nose bandages and ear bandages, not to speak of bandages hidden under their clothes.

I failed to recognize the swimmer, or paddler, in the pool, so I assumed he was a New Man. Women outnumber men greatly in institutions like ours, and new male residents are always welcomed as someone who puts the ratio in better balance. Whenever a man who appears to be single moves into Locksley Glen, he is referred to as the New Man until we get to know him.

I returned the New Man's greeting, and he introduced himself as Aidan. I told him I was Alice, called Alice One because another Alice had arrived at Locksley Glen after I did.

"Nice to meet you," he responded, with the obligatory reply, then resumed paddling. I followed suit, and we said no more. I thought I detected some kind of an accent in his speech, but I forgot about it, half-closed my eyes again and, while paddling gently, began a reverie.

My mind returned to the problem of the Wet Bathing Suit. What might have happened? I imagined a scene in which someone wearing that two-piece black swimsuit enters the pool, only to discover Chris Markel, the current film heartthrob, swimming there. The New Man appears, demanding that Chris, who is not a resident and not even a guest of a resident, leave immediately.

At that point the woman in the black bathing suit defends Chris's right to swim wherever he wants because of his status as a movie star. Chris smiles at me in appreciation (for I have suddenly become the woman in the black suit) and invites me to leave the pool with him and relax in the big basket chairs below the overhang. I know that there a ceiling fan will keep us cool. I hear splashing as we emerge and put on our beach coats.

Then I hear the New Man saying goodbye, and I realize that I have been in one of my reveries, that the splashing came from his exiting the pool. I find that I am sitting by myself in one of the basket chairs, wrapped in my short white beach cover. Peeking under the collar, I see only my old green bathing suit. No two-piece black job.

And no Chris Markel.

Sighing, I lifted my feet onto a footstool, closed my eyes, and fell asleep.

THREE

Because it was nearly time for our annual Locksley Glen Olympics, residents willing to expose themselves to ridicule signed up to join teams competing in a series of activities laughingly called physical.

For the Olympics, Activities Director Brett Bozeman chose competitions that were unashamedly easy even for elementary school.

Most of us had declined physically enough that we could no longer engage in standard activities like tennis or golf. Instead, we competed in tapping a golf ball into a small hole, throwing a basketball into a wastebasket, tossing a beanbag into a square box, and throwing a baseball a couple of yards. Running a race was, of course, out of the question. It involved an activity we hardly remembered performing, and we kept in mind the fervent hope that such performance would never become necessary.

There was also a sort of bowling game, in which participants tried to knock down some wooden pins with a small, light ball. During practice for this game, the ball often ended up on a table or in someone's lap. Or it just got lost. As for real bowling, the closest that competitors got to it was Wii Bowling, that virtual game presented with film and a computer—I never quite figured out how, even though I watched it done.

In Wii bowling, the participants stand facing the TV screen pretending to grasp an invisible bowling ball (a real one would be too heavy), and they swing their arms as if they are bowling, sometimes appearing in the film to knock down a few pins with their pretend ball.

I found this activity too unsatisfying to enjoy. I have seen some participants so taken with it that when they appeared to have made contact with the pins they jumped around with joy, or tried to jump around, sometimes hurting themselves as a result. They retire to their walkers or motorized chairs, chastened.

When I arrived at Locksley Glen three years ago, I was taken aback at the low level of physical effort needed to participate in such "Olympic" activities, but it wasn't long before I realized that my arthritic joints would no longer permit anything more strenuous than those scheduled by our compassionate activities director.

"We all have some infirmities," pointed out the resident named Starr, whom I met at that time, dressed for her putting contest in a striking black linen outfit of pleated shorts and sleeveless blouse, a costume more suited to a photo shoot for *Vogue* than to a physical competition.

I soon learned of Starr's physical limitation: one day at dinner she began coughing uncontrollably and rose to leave the table, but when Katrina made a move to follow her, Starr waved her off. In a few minutes Starr returned, but in her absence Katrina whispered to me, "She has COPD," which I learned were letters that referred to a complex of illnesses causing chronic difficulties in breathing.

At that time I didn't know Starr never wore any color but black—although technically, of course, black isn't a color… but never mind that. Artists should avoid correcting people's misunderstandings about color.

Subsequently, I discovered that when competing in the Olympics, Starr was supposed to wear the orange T-shirt indicating membership in her team, the Sharks, but she declined to wear something as prosaic as a T-shirt. "It would spoil the looks of my costume," I heard her declare. So while competing she tied the shirt around her waist by its sleeves, tearing it off immediately after.

We all have our quirks. Perhaps I have a few myself, although I can't think of any.

As a golf putter, Starr proved to be only fair, making a score of six out of ten tries, but even that low score helped her team beat the weak competition. I had been assigned to the Falcons, so I wore their purple shirt and in the putting competition made the less-than-notable score of three out of ten.

"Don't worry," Starr assured me, "the Locksley Glen Olympics includes stimulating mental activities as well as physical. You can sign up for games like bridge, poker, and mahjong, and competitions like solving crossword puzzles. We can't play 'What's My Line?' because we already know the line of everybody here: Retired. But we do have a version of 'Name That Tune' and 'Jeopardy,' and even a spelling contest, as in your standard second-grade match."

"Can't wait," I responded. "I did pretty well in second grade." And that first year at Locksley Glen I won the spelling contest. Well, after all, I was an English major. During the medal award ceremony, Brett Bozeman hung the gold-colored plastic Spelling Championship Medal around my neck with a red, white, and blue ribbon, and I marched to my seat very much pleased with myself.

See that? I told myself; just set your sights low enough, and you'll do fine.

This year I had volunteered for "Jeopardy" and the beanbag toss. During practice with throwing the beanbag, a competition I used to ace when I was a kindergartener, I made two out of ten tries. Not very good. In fact, pretty lame. If I had done that poorly in kindergarten, I might have flunked the course. So I pinned my hopes on "Jeopardy," a contest patterned after the successful television show of the same name.

Locksley Glen featured two game rooms, one large and one small. During our Olympics, both were constantly in use. While walking to the Small Game Room (where I never saw any small game) for this contest, I noticed that in a nearby patio a ball-throwing contest was proceeding. There the New Man was throwing with unexpected skill, smoothness, and accuracy. He had even attracted an audience, whose members oohed and aahed at his performance. I stopped to watch.

It was then I realized I had seen the New Man a few times before, in hallways or in the Dining Room. With clothes on, he looked more familiar. I knew then he was not as new as I had thought. He had probably been at Locksley Glen for a month or more.

Applause at the end of his show made the thrower remove the baseball cap he wore (heedless of his revelation of the Band-Aid on his bald head) and favor his audience with a slight bow. Then he sat down on a folding chair next to a gaunt-looking woman I had seen before but didn't know. She was gazing at him with a look of thrilled devotion. Some of the men clustered around him, competing for the privilege of praising him.

Something clicked in my brain, and I linked the name "Aidan" with baseball. This man, I finally realized, was Aidan MacCracken, a retired baseball player who was now a resident of Locksley Glen. He had played on professional teams in one of the big leagues as well as in the minors.

Aidan MacCracken had made the general news because as an immigrant from Scotland, he had never played the American National Game until he was eighteen. That's when his parents brought him to this country, and he learned baseball in college, somewhere around New York City.

I knew then why I had detected a slight accent on encountering him in the pool. Aidan MacCracken had been born in Scotland.

Suddenly I realized I was staring, and I turned away, only to run into Katrina and her boyfriend Bill Hufferman. Immediately, I noticed with dismay that Katrina wore The Boot, an ugly black foot-covering we were all familiar with.

To walk while wearing this detested object means to feel that one is dragging along a copy of the New York City Yellow Pages. Moreover, it has to be worn for at least three weeks whenever a foot or ankle is injured, an event that is regrettably frequent at Locksley Glen. The Boot looked particularly incongruous with Katrina's pink dress. "Good Heavens, Katrina, I didn't know you'd hurt your foot. Or did you wrench your ankle?"

"Just broke a small bone. So it's my turn to be sentenced to several weeks in The Footmonster. As if we didn't already have enough trouble walking." And she leaned on her walker.

"I'm so sorry. But your pretty pink gown cancels out our glimpse of the ugly Boot."

"Thanks. I always feel most comfortable in the Dutch national costume. Bill, as it happens, is suffering more than I am."

"What happened, Bill?"

"Tooth problems, which involve a couple of root canals," he remarked, frowning. "Most of the pain comes not from the canal-dredging but from Medicare's refusal to cover the huge cost of all this."

I nodded in sympathy. When we became seniors we accepted with joy the perk of Medicare's willingness to cover eighty percent of our health costs—until we discovered that our common and expensive age-related problems with our eyes, our ears, and our teeth are not covered at all. Our monthly Social Security checks fail to reach far enough to encompass the enormous cost of hearing aids, eyeglasses, and tooth repairs of any kind.

Growing old is not only bothersome, it's expensive.

After commiserating with Bill, I began to feel my own pain. I no longer felt up to competing in "Jeopardy" or anything else, so I retreated to the pool court to relax in a basket chair and feel sorry for myself for suffering with the arthritis in my back and other joints.

Before a minute was up I realized I had fallen into the self-pity syndrome I had criticized in others, so I roused myself to walk to my apartment and take a pain pill, after which I checked the schedule for the day in order to choose an activity to participate in.

Since I didn't feel like working on my painting, I would do something passive: attend a presentation by a florist who advised residents on houseplants we could try to raise in our apartments. She was scheduled to give a talk on how to care for these plants without killing them before Snowbird Season is over.

Feigning perfect health, as we often do, I walked briskly, or what passed for briskly at the Glen, to the Small Game Room, where Elise Parker, in her second presentation to us, presided not over small game but over a selection of beautiful houseplants, some of them in full bloom.

In her presentation the previous month, Elise had revealed her expertise by explaining how to select suitable houseplants for our apartments. That inspired many residents to show up for her follow-up lecture on how to care for them. The room was full. I slipped in and stood at the back so that I could view the scene without blocking anyone's view.

Elise was explaining, "If you are like Mrs. Hamm and enjoy growing plants on your porch—pardon me, I should use the local word *lanai*, not porch—you should keep the humid Florida atmosphere in mind and choose plants that do not care to be flooded with a sprinkling can full of water each day. With treatment like that, these plants may drown." She named some of the plants—they were called by names like

"rose mallow," "cardinal flower," and "summersweet" —
and then she went on: "These wonderful plants need only a
brief wetting."

Then Lucas walked in and stood next to me. At that point,
Elise happened to look up and notice him. She said, "Ah, Mr.
Ledbetter. Have you wet your plants today?"

Lucas's eyes grew round. He turned around and walked
out of the room.

I guess Lucas, too, has a hearing problem.

FOUR

My next glimpse of the New Man, Aidan MacCracken, came the day Joan and her husband Clarence invited him to join them when they went to the Dining Room for dinner. Beforehand, they were all drinking in a group that also included me.

Most residents like to gather at this time of day in the barroom (Its technical name is The Living Room.), where we can request wine or a cocktail concocted by the current drinksmeister, young Huberto, who is just barely of the age to touch liquor but who has somehow learned the skills requisite for creating good drinks.

When I approached the table where the group sat, the baseball player was questioning the accuracy of the name of our institution, Locksley Glen. I noticed that Bill Hufferman got a bit huffy when Aidan finished his query by saying, "What kind of a glen is this? Obviously, the person who named this place has never seen a real glen."

Bill, perhaps still suffering with tooth pain, bristled and responded, "Okay, so exactly what is a glen?"

"It's a wee valley, a narrow one. Your Locksley Glen seems to be a building, one constructed on flat land."

"It is," Bill responded. "It's an American glen, so don't expect anyone here to pipe in the haggis on Bobby Burns's birthday." I think Bill was a bit irked at all the attention Aidan MacCracken was getting. To smooth things over, Katrina asked where Aidan had played.

"A few big-league teams, but mostly in the minors. I played for a lot of PCL teams."

"PCL.... That stands for Pullman Car Lounge?" Bill asked. I'm afraid he was being a bit snarky.

"No," Joan said, thinking of her own explanation: "Pretty Cool Liquidators."

"This is fun," Katrina put in. Glancing at her foot, she said "Plaster Cast Legs."

"No," said Clarence. "Petty Cash Liberators."

By then we were all smiling and thinking of new explanations for those three letters. All of us except Aidan.

"Playing Card Lords," I contributed.

Then Aidan thought of something. "Partly-Covered Loins," he said.

And we all stopped, thinking this had gone on long enough. Perhaps a little too long. People our age generally shrink away from off-color jokes. They make us uncomfortable.

Clarence deflected more suggestions by declaring, "PCL stands for Pacific Coast League. Right, Aidan?"

"Yes. I need a refill."

As he left the table, we all tried to look elsewhere. Clarence finally made an uncharacteristically vulgar remark: "Somebody ought to give that guy a wedgie."

Joan looked at him with a shocked expression. Finally, she said, "Aidan seems to gravitate toward that gaunt-looking woman. Or she toward him. Anybody know her name?"

We had already noticed that the woman in question was drinking at the bar with Heather and Annabelle, but she kept throwing glances at our table, glances that seemed to be meant for Aidan. When he approached the bar, so did her glances.

"I'm going to dine with Annabelle at 5:15, if our table is ready," I announced. "I'll ask her who that woman is. She's been here a while, but I still don't know her name."

Aidan, who was to have dinner with Joan and Clarence, returned to our table, and Joan, determined to change the subject, asked me about the still life I was working on. I replied, "It's progressing more slowly than I hoped it would."

Aidan turned to me. "You're an artist?" I nodded, so he said, "I'm looking for someone to paint a portrait of my late wife."

I shook my head. "Sorry, I don't paint from photographs. I assume that's what you expected. But I never found that kind of work satisfying."

Aidan responded with a remark I didn't care for. "Well, since she's not alive, how else could you paint her?"

Obviously, this man expects me to cater to him, I thought, and I resolved to stand my ground. "I would not be able to handle the assignment, although I'm sure you could find other artists in Naples to take the commission."

"Commission?"

"Yes." After a slight pause, I added, "Did you think I work for free?"

"I guess I did. After all, painting is hardly a job. More like a hobby."

This time I bristled. "Painting is my life work, the way I have made my living, along with lecturing about art history." Then sitting forward, I thought of another remark: "Maybe playing a game is more like a hobby." Thoroughly annoyed, I got up and left.

I saw Annabelle approaching. She addressed me: "Let's go and check on our table.... What's the matter? You look upset."

"I just lost my temper and told off the New Man. I'm a bit ashamed of myself."

"What? You shaved yourself? It's very noisy here."

"Annabelle, let's wait till we are seated to talk."

At the table, before I could even examine the menu, Annabelle began talking about her daughter Corliss, who was nagging her to leave Locksley Glen and come to live with her and her husband in Denver.

Annabelle explained, "I love my daughter, but what in the world would I do in Denver? I don't know anyone in that part of the country.

"Corliss is insisting I come live in her big, beautiful home, where I would have a suite of my own. She says Naples is too far for her to come whenever I get sick. She's right, of course. I can't expect that."

"But Annabelle, this is your home. Here among your friends. You've been here for years."

She began to look distraught, and I knew she was torn between wanting to please her daughter and wanting to continue the life she had made at Locksley Glen, where she played mahjong every day, enjoyed the monthly lunch excursions, and took part in poker, chair exercises, and craft work.

Annabelle and her friend Heather were drawn to the same activities and usually participated together in whatever was going on. They even attended the monthly beach picnics, although walking on sand had become difficult for them and almost all of us. I often thought what a sight we must be as we staggered along the beach, trying to walk on something that gave way when we stepped on it.

"Your daughter doesn't need to come here when you get sick. All the Locksley Glen aides are ready to take care of you."

"I hate to question my daughter's judgment. Maybe, at this stage of my life, it's better than my own." She began twisting the napkin on her lap.

"Why do you think that? You know what makes you happy: it's being among your friends."

"But I'm getting so old. Maybe I'll die here." Her voice wobbled, and tears formed in her eyes.

"Maybe this is the best place to die."

Silence, while we both thought about this. Gingerly.

"Without my daughter?"

"Is it necessary for her to see your final moments?"

Silence again.

"Not really. I saw my husband's, and the experience was terribly painful for me. I can't forget it."

"Remember what happened when Rosa moved to her daughter's home in New Jersey?"

Pause. "She kept phoning Mary One and complaining that her daughter was too busy to spend time with her."

"Rosa's daughter had her own life. Rosa was developing one here, and she missed it terribly when she left it. How will you do without friends like Heather? And doesn't your daughter Corliss have a job, where she works away from home?"

Annabelle nodded. Just then the young waiter Bertrand came to take our orders. About time, I thought, then inwardly berated myself for being critical. I turned to Bertrand with a pleasant face, but not before patting Annabelle's hand briefly to show my concern for her dilemma.

While we ate our salads, we talked of lighter things. Annabelle said she and Heather had made friends with the gaunt-looking woman, who came from New York and was named Shelley Pace.

Annabelle brightened as she shared the news that Shelley was already acquainted with Aidan McCracken. Shelley had actually dated Aidan years ago, when he played in New York. "I think she was a member of a fan club. Maybe she was a groupie. She said she was known as a 'Baseball Annie.'"

My eyebrows rose. I knew the phrase. My husband had once explained to me that it indicated close attachment to a player and sometimes meant cohabitation.

"Wow!" I said. "She *was* a groupie." I almost used the phrase "camp follower," which is thoroughly negative, but in the nick of time I decided I could not judge Shelley Pace's choices in life. Not all of my own have been wise.

Just then a rumble of raised voices came from the Living Room, where about twenty people were still drinking. Annabelle and I thought little of it, but while we were having our broiled salmon, we heard a distant siren and saw the flashing lights of the Naples Fire and Rescue Department's vehicle. By then we knew that another Locksley Glen resident had suddenly become very sick or had fallen. But at dessert time I was distracted, and much entertained, when Annabelle ordered "Burberry pie," and the server, who came from Colombia, inexplicably knew exactly what she wanted.

It was not until the next morning that Handsome Harry's assistant, Polly Trevette, revealed to a group of us talking in the hall that Heather had been taken to the hospital, where she was pronounced dead on arrival.

Heather! Our own dear Heather.

I resolved never again to give advice to anyone considering leaving the Glen to live with family. Especially my opinions on where to do your dying.

This resolution would last about as long as other resolutions I've made in the past.

FIVE

We were seated on the bus taking us to a local museum when we realized we would need to give solace to our friend Annabelle, who found herself unable to stop talking to her seatmate, Katrina, about losing her friend Heather.

"I'm not going to make friends with any of these people ever again," we heard her say with a shaky voice, "because they'll only die on me. It's too painful." Annabelle couldn't prevent a sob from rising out of her misery, although Katrina had her arm around our suffering friend to comfort her.

I suddenly remembered stories about the way soldiers withdrew from friendships with their wartime comrades when they realized that those comrades might die and cause them the pain of losing someone they loved. Annabelle feels the same way, I realized. We already have enough pain, physical and psychological, and desire fervently to avoid more of the same. Instead, we look for fun.

Just then the Locksley Glen bus lurched, as Jerry the Driver tried to avoid hitting a wayward Muscovy duck that made the mistake of hesitating on its way to a pond on the other side of the road. Annabelle, who had neglected to fasten her seat belt, tipped dangerously to one side. If Katrina hadn't been holding her, Annabelle, in her distracted state, might have slid off the seat.

"Oh! Katrina. Thank you. You're always so kind to me."

"Not at all, Annabelle. Let me help you get fastened. And let's try to think of some positive things about our situation. Think of why we came here in the first place."

Then Katrina brought her intellect to bear on the problem.

"We came because living alone can be dangerous as well as lonely, and because people no longer live in nineteenth-century style, with lots and lots of family members all living in the same house. In former days, only Papa worked outside the home. Nowadays, all the adults work. The young people form satellite families and move out, sometimes accepting jobs that require them to live half a world away from their parents and grandparents. And often they move again and again, as required by their careers.

"Did you read that interview with the actor Nick Nolte? He said that the hardest thing to accept in growing old is seeing your children become so involved in their own lives that they drift away. We find it difficult to accept that they have to put their own families and responsibilities first. We cannot expect anything else. They must organize their lives so that their immediate families come first.

"But we must do the same—put ourselves first.

"So we turn to places like Locksley Glen. This kind of residence isn't just a place to stay. It's a place for living our own personal lives. Here we can decide what we want to do with our time: perhaps by continuing some of our former activities? By taking up new interests? It's up to us. It's our life to live, and we should value the opportunity.

"Think of what you want to accomplish. Focus on that rather than on what others may think is appropriate. Downplay the role of physical problems that plague us. Try not to give pain center stage. Isn't there some new adventure you'd like to try?"

In her intensity, Katrina, with her silvery hair braided into a crown, began to seem to me like a statue of a kindly angel. I verged on relaxing into an alternative adventure featuring a benevolent spirit, then shook it off and pulled myself back to reality.

How wise Katrina is, I thought. She sees this stage of life as less a problem than an opportunity. That's her psychological training kicking in. I respected the abilities that had earned her a doctorate in her field.

I saw Annabelle begin to nod in agreement. She was starting to think of her situation in a new way. "Yes, there are some new things I want to try. I guess I must begin to live for myself, in my own way."

Next to me on the van sat Joyce Joslin, whose oxygen line to her nostrils had been partly dislodged by the swerve, but she pushed it back into position.

Joyce, I realized, never complained about the heart problems that made it necessary for her to lug an oxygen tank wherever she went. Instead, Joyce slung it over one shoulder and kept her attention on other things. She spent time on a quilting project, which she had started to steer her mind away from the recent tragic death of her only son in a plane accident. I could see, from the smidgen of colorful material peeking out of Joyce's handbag, that she carried her work with her and added to it whenever the opportunity arose.

Just as I prepared to ask Joyce about her quilt, we arrived at the Collier County Museum, where Brett Bozeman had reserved a docent to explain the exhibits to us. Jerry the Driver pulled out his traveling footstool and placed it at the bottom of the van's steps, where we availed ourselves of his helping hand for dismounting. Each of us tried to suppress the grunts of pain that stepping downward elicited because of fractured spinal discs, worn-out knees, degenerating hips, and the ever-present arthritis.

Behind me I could hear the gaunt woman, Shelley Pace, talking to Bob Avery, her seatmate on the van, as they approached the line of people ready to enter the museum. "And do you own a cellphone?" she was asking.

"I have a saxophone. Does that count?" was Bob's reply. Bob's unruly hair, I noticed, stood up in large spikes because of the damp weather, and he was trying to smooth it down. Dagwood Bumstead, I thought.

As if he had been listening to my thoughts, Bob turned to me. "Did you bring any of that Harvey's Bristol Cream you like, Alice One?" he joked, continuing to run his hand over his head.

"It wouldn't flatten your hair, if that's what you have in mind," I replied, smiling. "It isn't that kind of cream."

"Maybe it would help Aidan," Bob quipped. Our baseball resident hadn't shown up for this trip.

Bob's reference to the ball player's bald head elicited a defensive response from Shelley Pace. "He wasn't always bald, you know. He had a full head of brown hair when I met him."

"When was that, Shelley?" Bob asked as we began walking toward the museum.

"Back in the '40s."

"The *nineteen*-forties?"

No reply to this impertinent remark was forthcoming, perhaps because our attention was drawn to the docent, who came out of the building to introduce herself as Ellen Copperthwaite.

Ellen led us onward into the first room of the museum, with its displays relating to settlers of European descent who in the 1800s began moving into what became Collier County.

And this is where the idea came to me that soon began torturing us. No doubt I have too vivid an imagination, but when the idea came to me, it infected others, too.

After explaining the history of the European settlers, Ellen showed us a room with striking photos of mummified bodies of very early residents, the aborigines. Their bodies had been preserved by having fallen into a swampy area that contained calcifying elements. We learned that these mummies had been salvaged from a place called Bone Valley.

The photos were really a bit horrifying, especially to old people like us, and we tried to move out of that room as quickly as possible without insulting Ellen, the docent.

But on the threshold of the next room I stopped short. "I just thought of something," I said to Bob, the nearest person. "What if the wet bathing suit left at the pool belonged on a person's body... a body that was once alive but is now dead?"

Bob was taken aback. "Don't think like that, Alice One. That would mean we might have a murderer at the Glen."

"Murderer?" said Joyce. "Couldn't be. Could it?"

"All I can think of these days is death," contributed Annabelle. "I wouldn't be surprised."

Suddenly I realized that Shelley, who had overheard this conversation, was turning pale. "Shelley," I suggested, "maybe you'd better sit down for a moment."

"Yes, I will." She moved into the next room, where she sank onto a bench between an old wooden liquor keg and an iron stove, items left over from the 1800s that the museum had placed on display. "Low blood pressure," she explained, her voice muffled because she had lowered her head to her lap. "I'm better now."

"But there couldn't have been a murder," I asserted, reversing my position. "The Glen keeps careful track of where residents are, because it's legally responsible for our well-being. Nobody is missing... or... is someone missing that we don't know about?"

Bob thought for a moment, then pointed out, "Two people recently went on trips: Marge O'Doul, to visit for three weeks with her family in the Boston area; and the jewelry designer Hermione Kreutzer, who always spends two summer months in Virginia with her son and his family. Anybody heard from them?"

We were silent.

SIX

Iwas still thinking about the two absent residents as I got my clothing ready for the Labor Day picnic on the beach. The Glen tradition is to wear shorts and T-shirts on Labor Day, although some of us who are sensitive about the appearance of our legs demur and put on trousers. We are unwilling to expose our old legs to view.

Our activities director schedules monthly beach picnics — that is, for those who want to make the effort to walk on sand that frighteningly gives way to nothingness when foot pressure is put on it — but the Labor Day picnic is more elaborate.

On Labor Day the beach picnic includes a little ceremony in which workers are recognized. Moreover, some people attempt to make the day into a festive occasion by trying to play volleyball, despite the actual impossibility of such an occurrence. Lucas always staggers around a bit, trying to reach the ball that Ed Champion has almost hit over the net, but they usually give up in about five minutes.

Nevertheless, the Labor Day picnic remains a popular occasion, one in which Locksley Glen residents can enjoy the illusion of participating in the kind of festivities they enjoyed in the past.

As it happened, I missed this year's picnic because of intense pain in a knee that some time ago had borne the brunt of a fall. Pain pills hardly helped, so I put my beach outfit away and stayed home. But I heard later, at Happy Hour, that while a group of my friends were collecting shells, Joan and Clarence reported to them on what they had done to discover clues to the question of the Wet Bathing Suit.

They had interviewed Polly Trevette, Handsome Harry's assistant, who kept track of where residents were supposed to be. Polly insisted that the two women Joan and Clarence were inquiring about were on bona fide trips to visit family members and had left their relatives' contact information with her department's secretary, as per regulations.

"Have you heard from either of them, Polly?" Clarence asked.

"Well, no, but we don't usually hear from residents while they're away. They sometimes phone here to talk to their friends, but not to us in the office. I haven't heard any resident say he or she heard from Marge or from Hermione. That's not unusual. But now you're starting to make me worry about them." Polly blinked nervously.

"Would you consider phoning them to check on whether they're all right?" inquired Joan.

"I'll have to ask Director Grambling if I could take such a step. He might prefer that I not disturb them. And, after all, there's no real reason to think they're not where they said they'd be. Is there?"

"Could you ask Grambling now?" Clarence pressed her.

"Oh, no. He's on vacation himself. In Bermuda. He hates to be contacted while he's trying to relax." More blinking was in evidence.

"So who's minding the store?" Joan said lightly.

"What?"

"Who's in control here while Director Grambling is Relaxing In Bermuda?"

"Why, Mrs. Appletree herself, of course. The owner. I'm sure she would fail to see the necessity for long-distance calls just to be sure people were where they said they'd be. Mrs. Appletree is very conservative about taking actions of that sort." Blink, blink.

"Hmm. Yes. Okay."

And that was as far as Joan and Clarence could get on the matter of missing residents.

At least the picnic proved to be a pleasant one, according to Joan. Only one person fell while trying to walk on the beach: Clarence. Luckily, he didn't break anything and was immediately helped up by Brett Bozeman, having suffered only a sore tailbone. That injury failed to affect his appetite for the fried chicken, his favorite part of the celebration.

It was the day after the Labor Day picnic when Ed Champion brought up an idea that at first seemed completely unrelated to our worries. But, as we soon discovered, it offered us an entirely new clue, something based on information in our monthly newsletter.

Each month we all received copies of *GleNewsletter*, which a clerk distributed to us through our internal mailboxes. This publication enabled Director Grambling to announce anything he wanted us all to know, like the dates of concerts and parties.

It warned us, for example, about the remodeling and updating of the kitchen, which slowed Dining Room service. It explained his decision to have a tree cut down when it started to grow into a resident's window. And it reminded us that when the fire alarm began screeching, we were to remain calm and wait for instructions (if it was merely a drill) or for help in getting from our apartments to the sidewalks outside (if it happened to be real). We were to avoid rushing around the halls excitedly, thus disturbing residents who had become psychologically fragile.

We all looked forward to these newsletters, especially to finding typographical errors, misspellings, and grammatical goofs that we could criticize. Discovering such lapses made us feel superior. And that's a good feeling. How often does that happen to people in their eighties or nineties?

A few months ago Director Grambling had decided to ask a resident to contribute to *The GleNewsletter* a column in which he or she interviewed another resident about that person's background, jobs, and accomplishments. The director called this column a "Sketch of a Resident," *sketch* being a word I preferred to reserve for my own field, art, and not share with writers. But I managed to keep to myself any critical remarks about this inaccurate and inept usage.

Because Barbie Boobs possessed considerable background in writing and publishing (aside from possessing two other considerable things), Director Grambling asked her to prepare these "sketches." Her first one proved to interest us inordinately.

Barbie chose to interview and write about a quiet couple we referred to privately as the Tall Swedes, both of them large, fair, square, and involved only in each other. Like some other couples, they preferred being Alone Together. They took all their meals at tables designed for two and avoided social events as much as practicable. Although we went along with their obvious wish for privacy, their behavior made us curious about them, so we planned to read Barbie's interview with close attention.

Ed Champion stopped me on my way home from an exercise class to talk about the Tall Swedes. He had just read Barbie's article.

"It seems that the Tall Swedes aren't even Swedish; they're Norwegian-American with the surname Berglund, and their given names are Astrid and Anders," Ed revealed.

I waited to learn what else Ed had discovered because I could tell from his posture and his grin that something was on his mind. Almost right away I learned that what excited Ed was the news that Barbie Boobs had uncovered Astrid's work experience.

"You'll never guess what position she used to hold," Ed said, and then grinned.

"Can I buy a vowel?" I inquired. That was a bit pert, as well as a worn-out remark, but I hate trying to guess the unguessable.

"None other than bathing suit model!"

"Bathing suit.... So maybe Astrid was the one! The one who left a wet bathing suit in the pool area and walked away without it," I said happily.

"And maybe," he added, his triumph making him slip partly into his Kentucky accent, "theah is no dead body, just a discahded bathin' suit, left there caylessly by someone who probably has a closet full of those outfits."

"This discovery puts a different light on the subject. But... I've just thought of something. Isn't that black bathing suit rather small? Astrid Berglund is not small. She must be a size 14. What do you think?"

"I think we'll have to find out."

"So are you going to ask her?"

"Mmm. Maybe. If I get the nerve," he ventured. Or I'll ask a woman to find out. I'll bet Annabelle would do it. She's a neighbor of mine. No, a neighbor of Lucas's, I think. I'll get him to ask Annabelle to... what was it, again?"

We reviewed the task Ed had taken on, whatever it was. I can't recall. I was concentrating on mine. "I'll go check the size of the black bathing suit. I'm sure it's still in the Lost and Found box at the front desk. Maybe I'll learn something." And I marched away on this serious and important assignment: to dispel the need for some of these "maybes."

On my way I began thinking of the strange name we gave to that box full of items people had found. Why do we call it "Lost and Found?" If we look inside it, we find that it contains only Found items. They weren't Lost, although they used to be.

This insight seemed quite brilliant.

Before I could savor it, the fire alarm rang. It rang and rang and rang. Those of us not in our apartments tried to get home, in case aides arrived to tell us what to do. Those of us already in our apartments peeked into the hallway to find out what was happening.

As I passed Shelley Pace's apartment, she was peeking out, and I noticed she was wearing a robe... no, a sort of caftan made of a shiny material like taffeta. She held it together at the neck with her left hand, as if it was about to fall open. When she saw me, instead of greeting me she withdrew quickly, seemingly not wanting me to know she was there.

A caftan in the middle of the day?

I filed that information away for later consideration. Like Scarlett, I planned to think about that tomorrow.

I found ear plugs in the top drawer of my bedroom chest, inserted them, and sat down to read the local paper. There was no use trying to work on my still life with all that racket going on. Ear plugs merely muted the noise. When the ringing finally ceased, I closed my eyes, hoping to lower my blood pressure.

Suddenly, I was in one of my visions of alternate reality, a vision of a woman cowering in front of a strong man who was pulling a black bathing suit off her body while she tried unsuccessfully to fight him off.

I was shocked at the intensity of the vision and managed to extract myself from it quickly. I figured out what had brought this on. The problem of the Wet Bathing Suit was lurking in my subconscious without my realizing it, underscored by a scene in that Chris Markel movie.

I took a few deep breaths and drank some water. Then it occurred to me to check the director's newsletter, so I read the story Barbie Boobs had prepared about the Norwegian couple. I found that it contained other interesting details, like the name of Astrid's employer.

Although she and her husband had both worked in California, she was unconnected with the film industry or with Silicon Valley, which was too recent a development to jibe with her employment history anyway. Astrid had worked as a model for a beachwear company that published a popular catalog called *Boardwalk Beachwear*.

I recalled having seen that catalog back in the '60s. The company offered various models of bathing suits from the ultra-conservative one-piecers with swingy skirts or "boy shorts" to two-piece models designed to appeal to women younger or slightly more daring than I was. A variety of beach coats, sun hats, and flip-flop shoes helped fill the pages.

So Astrid had been one of the voluptuous models parading through that catalog in exotic-looking bathing apparel! It's strange the way we sometimes meet in later life people we've had some kind of contact with many years earlier.

By then I felt ready to return to work on my still life. I forgot about my plan to check the size of the bathing suit in the Lost and Found box. Instead, I began mixing the colors of paint I needed and then, consulting my sketches, I picked up work on the painting where I had left off. It was six o'clock when I realized I had nearly missed dinner, so I hastened to clean up.

SEVEN

Having worked late the previous evening, I failed to awaken next morning at my regular time and arrived at breakfast later than usual. Looking around, I saw no seats available next to people I knew, so I walked over to some residents I hadn't been introduced to and asked if I could join them. They welcomed me, so I sat down and identified myself as Alice One, so-called because of being the earliest Alice to arrive at Locksley Glen.

I heard all five of their names given, and I even kept them in mind for about five minutes, but the only name I remembered later was Hugh, borne by a big man with thick eyebrows and wearing a tan corduroy jacket. Those brows made him look formidable, since he had a habit of dipping his chin down and then looking up at us through the ample shrubbery above his eyes.

His habit caused me to turn away from him, for I suddenly recalled a photo of C.J. Jung in a biography of the psychoanalyst, a photo in which Jung, with chin down, looked up through his heavy eyebrows in this same scary way.

The result was that my first impression of Hugh was to be a bit frightened of him.

The chattiest person at the table, a woman with her gray hair twisted upward in an elegant bun, talked about the previous night's Bingo winners, a bicycle accident she read about in the local paper, how much her arthritis hurt, and the terrible disease her great-aunt died of. Hugh talked about football. The others just listened or ate as Ms. Chatty and Hugh prattled on, speaking mostly to themselves.

Then I noticed that Aidan was at the next table. He glanced over at me several times, not smiling or nodding. In fact, his looks were quite malevolent.

Well, I thought to myself, we had a disagreement, but there's no need to be mean about it.

"...and have you had your cataracts removed, too, Alice One?" Chatty's less than riveting question penetrated my consciousness I mustered my politeness and replied briefly, resolving to leave as soon as possible.

Walking home, I felt quite put out by Aidan's obvious animosity. Is he really angry at me? Is he, in fact, likely to do me some harm? He could certainly hurt me if he had a mind to; he's still athletic and strong, even if he is in the last quarter of his life.

I could feel my blood pressure rising, so I decided to delay a return to my painting and instead take some relaxation at one of my favorite places in Locksley Glen, the pool patio.

Sinking into one of the comfortable basket chairs facing the pool, I took some deep breaths.

Perhaps I'm imagining the intensity of Aidan's anger toward me, I thought. Focusing on the sound of water splashing from a pipe into the pool, I began watching the surface water change and ripples fan out from the center. I was alone, and soon I was relaxed.

But my imagination continued to work. Suddenly my mind conjured up a vision of a body in a swamp. Naked, of course. Female. A bit shrunken, but still identifiably female. And old, like us. The person who had just put the body in the swamp appeared to be a man in a heavy black cloak, which he'd used to cover the body as he transported it there, but now he wore it as a partial disguise.

As I looked at this man in my vision, he appeared familiar. He was strong, for his muscles moved under the cloak as he took it from the body and wrapped himself in it.

Who was he? Hugh? Aidan? And what motive would he have to kill a woman? Maybe he got rid of all his conquests that way.

If he was Aidan, that wouldn't be true, for Aidan didn't get rid of Shelley Pace. Why did I think it might be Hugh, whom I hardly knew?... Ah! It was coming to me. An article in the previous day's *New York Times* told an unsavory story: a football player named Hugh Houseman had deliberately hurt his girlfriend and put her in the hospital. That article still bothered me.

I remained for a time under the influence of that vision: I can't see under the cloak, but it couldn't be Hugh. Maybe it's Aidan after all. Is Aidan the Wet Bathing Suit bad guy? Could he be angry enough to kill someone? I doubt it. Aidan seems like a civilized man. After all, what would the motive be?

I must erase this vision, I told myself. Maybe there was no bad guy, and the Wet Bathing Suit wasn't a clue to anything at all. It was just a discarded piece of clothing. No doubt I was imagining something sinister where there was nothing of the sort.

"Hi, Alice One! I'm back!" Opening my eyes, I saw Starr, wearing a black cotton sleeveless jump suit with oversize white beads and carrying a copy of *People* magazine. She sat down in a basket chair, shook her feet to remove her (banned for residents here) flip-flops, and peeped at me over large-windowed dark sunglasses.

"Back? You were away?"

"You didn't miss me? I was in Washington, D.C., for almost a week. Got back yesterday."

"But... we didn't know. Did you tell Polly Trevette?"

"Who bothers with that? Besides, I didn't want everyone to know I was visiting a man." She grinned mischievously.

"You're incorrigible. What if you'd had one of your COPD attacks?"

"Washington has hospitals. The man I visited would have taken care of me. But, ah, those restaurants in Washington! And the exciting atmosphere—I love it! What a vital city...."

I interrupted her with a request. "Starr, will you do something for me? I need to sketch a body pose."

"Pose? You want me to pose for you?"

"Just one leg. That's all I need." I whipped out my sketchbook and charcoal pencil, which I usually keep in my purse. "Will you stand over here and put one leg forward, as if you were walking?"

"Sure. Like this?"

"I need to sketch the back leg. Will you pull up the pants on that leg?"

Starr giggled and complied. "I feel like Claudette Colbert in 'It Happened One Night.'"

"Stay like that while I make a few sketches." And I worked at recording the pose, moving my view from one angle to another until Starr got tired—about three minutes. "Thanks. I've got it."

"So this is a one-legged painting you're working on?"

I smiled. "You'll see later. You can sit down now."

"Well, when I was away, did I miss anything?"

"We're still trying to figure that out." Suddenly I remembered that I was going to check on the size of the lost-and-found bathing suit to find out whether it would fit the ex-model named Astrid Berglund.

"Come with me. I'll explain later."

On the way, Starr talked about Washington's museums and the crowded airplanes she'd used. Because of her connection with a travel agency, she knew how to get marvelous deals, but I wasn't particularly interested in her remarks until she added, "I got home early yesterday in time to join the group at this month's beach picnic. Where were you? That ballplayer, Aidan, was there, and so was Shelley Pace."

"I was hurting. Did you all have a pleasant time?"

"Well, Aidan didn't. He told several of us that he was disappointed that none of the women wore bathing suits."

"Really?"

"Sure. When he saw that we just wore slacks or shorts and blouses, he muttered, "What kind of a beach picnic is this?" then walked away and picked up a few shells. He sat on a log, and when Shelley walked over there to join him, he got up and took another walk."

EIGHT

"Where are you two going? Come have lunch with us. We want to talk to you," said Clarence. I supposed my errand could wait—it had already done that for a while. So Starr and I followed Clarence and his wife Joan into the Dining Room. As we sat down, I suddenly started to laugh.

"What? Is something funny?" Joan queried.

"I'm just thinking of the day Clarence claimed he was the owner of the black bathing suit and had used palm fronds to fill the upper part."

"It raises a wonderful picture in the mind," Joan agreed, and we all grinned foolishly.

"Listen," demanded Clarence, "I think I can clear up a misperception. I know that the story about the Norwegian woman named Astrid made people think that Astrid, since she'd been a bathing suit model, had left one of her many bathing suits at the pool. But I can't see that argument, because the suit left in the pool patio is not the type of suit that her company produced."

"What? How do you know?"

"When I ran a department store, my purchasing agent occasionally bought beachwear from that company on a wholesale basis. The suits produced by Boardwalk Beachwear had the reputation of being extremely sexy, even vulgar— like postage stamps on strings—so we bought sparingly from them. Thongs and straps didn't sell well in Indianapolis."

"Nonsense," I said.

"What's nonsense?"

"I bought from Boardwalk Beachwear's retail catalog, and I don't remember seeing anything sexy at all. I always ordered the fitted one-piece suits with princess styling—slightly flared skirts. Nothing especially sexy about them. The two-piece suit left in our pool patio looks like the full-coverage outfits I saw in Boardwalk Beachwear's retail catalog, which carried no bikinis or thongs. Some of the suits even had overskirts, to wear on the beach. They were designed to be removed when the wearer entered the water."

"A BLT, please," said Joan to Maurizio, the server who had been hovering over our table while Clarence and I were disagreeing. Meanwhile, Joan muttered about being late for her daily walk.

"I'm stumped," said Clarence. "Uh, bring me the house salad, please."

"Salad for me, too," I said. "How can we remember that company's goods so differently?"

"Swiss on rye and applesauce on the side," said Starr. "So why don't we go check on the maker of that bathing suit?"

"Yes, let's. Maybe it has *Boardwalk Beachwear* sewed into the seam. And maybe it doesn't."

"That's a great idea."

"Besides, I promised yesterday to check the size of that bathing suit to see if it's large enough for a woman like Astrid to get into it."

Suddenly, we all felt some urgency for the project, so we had just barely finished chewing when we left for the front desk, where the person currently in charge, Kelley Conners, was answering a phone call: "This is Locksley Glen. How may I help you?"

The phone call proved to be a long one, and Clarence began to get impatient. He started pacing. Soon he was tapping on the counter with his fingernails. Joan mumbled something about needing to change into her purple running shoes and departed for her afternoon walk. That left Starr and me to contend with her jumpy husband and a long-winded telephoner.

Kelley, trying to concentrate on answering the phoned-in questions but increasingly nervous about Clarence's behavior, began flashing us frightened glances. I had never seen Clarence act this way, but Starr took me aside to explain his behavior.

She murmured that Joan had revealed to her that Clarence was showing disturbing signs of bipolar disorder. Apparently, the behavior I was witnessing supported that diagnosis.

Finally, Kelley gave us her attention and uttered the welcome words, "May I help you, Mr...."

By then Clarence was pounding on the counter and saying loudly, "The bathing suit! I want to see the bathing suit!"

Kelley backed away, then turned into the walk-in closet behind her.

Starr was trying to calm Clarence: "Remember your blood pressure. Take a few deep breaths."

Clarence was grinding his teeth.

Luckily, Kelley knew what Clarence meant when he demanded the bathing suit, and she brought out the Lost and Found box, setting it on the counter as an invitation for Clarence to find what he was looking for.

He plunged his hands into the box, rummaged around, came up with a black scarf, got stabbed in the finger by a pearl pin, and finally — finally! — brought out the black bathing suit, but he was too jumpy to find the label. Starr took over ("I'll do it, Clarence") and found the seam with the label.

"It says, "SuBe.com, Corona del Mar, Cal., Size 14.""

"SuBe.com," Clarence repeated. "What's that?"

Kelley came to life. "It means Sunny Beaches, the name of the swimsuit company. It's where I buy my suits. Online. Sunny Beaches dot com."

"Sunny Beaches. Not Boardwalk Beachwear?"

"No, sir. Boardwalk Beachwear has different styling. More expensive, too. The models look kind of snooty. It used to carry only conservative stuff, but now it carries colors like neon orange, styles like straps and bikinis, and thongs, too. My sister wears thongs, but I hate them — so uncomfortable. Is that all, sir?"

He nodded, suddenly looking tired. "I think I'll go take a nap," he announced. Looking wonderingly at Starr and me, he asked, "How could I have been so wrong?"

"I was wrong, too, Clarence. I didn't realize that Boardwalk Beachwear now carries more up-to-date swimsuits. I haven't bought a suit in years."

Starr and I walked with Clarence to his apartment just down the hall from the Front Desk.

"At least," I said to Starr when Clarence's door had closed, "we now know that Astrid could have worn that suit. Even if it wasn't made by the company she used to work for. Size 14 is considered a 'plus' size. Although it's the size I wear myself," I added ruefully. "Obviously, 'plus' indicates 'larger than average.'"

Starr turned to me. "You wear a 14? Better not tell anybody. They'll begin to suspect *you*."

Starr's comment startled me. More than that, it scared me, for everyone knew of my visions of alternate reality. Did they also realize that I sometimes come out of them not knowing where I have been or what I have done?

But I smiled at Starr and left her.

Then I had a call from Hugh of the Heavy Eyebrows, the man I had met at a recent breakfast. Re-introducing himself, he said that after learning I was an artist, he had asked around for my last name so he could look up my phone number on the Residents' List.

He said he needed some advice.

"I've visited several downtown art galleries on Third Street and picked out two paintings I like, but I'd appreciate your opinion on which might be worth my investment. Would you be able to join me on a short drive into town tomorrow afternoon to visit Patricia Knightsbridge's gallery?"

At that point, Hugh was obviously unaware that Patricia handles my work.

I wondered if I was wrong to accept Hugh's offer of a trip into town. Was I just putting myself in danger? Each time I pictured Hugh, I saw him looking at me from under those heavy eyebrows.

I decided to chance it.

NINE

A lthough I tried not to consider it, my mind refused to relinquish the worry about my visions. I kept thinking of the day when I had emerged from my revision of events at the pool, a drama in which Aidan was an actor. On coming out of that reverie I had found myself no longer in the pool but seated in a basket chair. I had no recollection of getting there.

While thinking of this problem, I stumbled as I walked over the threshold of the Mail Room but caught myself before losing my balance entirely.

Pay attention, I said to myself, or you will suffer a fall, like so many others. Think about visions later.

The mail in my box included an ad from an audiologist who wanted to sell me hearing aids. I didn't need a reminder that my hearing abilities are in decline. I also found a catalog from a clothing company advertising sleeveless dresses, ones that would expose my arms, which had recently developed a resemblance to old women's arms.

I flipped through the catalog. The shortness of the skirts on those dresses was remarkable and made them look as though the designer had forgotten to complete them. These beautiful dresses were of course displayed on skinny, 20-year-old models in three-inch heels.

Does anybody sell attractive dresses suitable for women my age? I wondered for the umpteenth time. No wonder so many of us settle for trousers and long-sleeved blouses.

Sighing with frustration, I went home and decided to forget clothes and get to work.

I was mixing some paints for flesh-color tones and thinking, "This will be an unusual still life!" when my worries came back to me, and I had to relinquish the paint brush while I considered the possible consequences of my visions.

Could it be that I owned the black bathing suit myself, removed it after swimming, and left it at the pool? Although I failed to recognize the suit as mine, I reluctantly admitted to myself that it might belong to me. Some of my clothing is old, and I seldom wear it, though I find it hard to give up favorite things.

Over the years we become closely attached to our belongings. That's why it's so hard to downsize our worldly goods when we move from a full-sized house to an apartment in assisted living. Some of us discover, to our dismay, that furniture we have loved for a long time will no longer fit in our new homes, and even worse, that nobody wants it. I remember when Annabelle...

Annabelle! She's the one I should be worried about. She's torn between staying at Locksley Glen and moving to Denver. She needs to figure out, as Katrina said, how to live the rest of her life.

I made up my mind to be Annabelle's sounding board. I phoned her, but she didn't feel like talking. I suggested dinner on the following day. What did discarded bathing suits matter when a decision like Annabelle's needed making?

Then it was time to meet Hugh.

TEN

Hugh pulled up to the front door of Locksley Glen in the white Toyota he'd told me to watch for and came out to open the car door for me. Wearing the ubiquitous tan sport coat, he approached smiling while lowering his chin. This alteration in his appearance made an entirely different impression on me. No longer did he seem frightening. As I slowly lifted my arthritic legs into the car, I felt a worry recede.

In another way, Hugh remained the same: he was still a talker. He reviewed for me his interest in art, not as an artist but as a person who appreciated art and particularly enjoyed museums, and he asked if I had seen the art museums in Philadelphia, Chicago, and Boston. We talked of MOMA in New York and even about the Uffizzi Galleria in Florence. I wondered why I had assumed he knew only about football, something I have no interest in. Perhaps I'm prone to making false assumptions.

Like those about the owner of the Wet Bathing Suit.

By the time we approached Patricia Knightsbridge's gallery, he had started to ask about my own work. "I've been gabbing about my own artistic interests instead of getting a real artist to tell me about her work. What kind of paintings do you produce?"

"I do representational work. Patricia Knightsbridge handles it."

"Why, that's wonderful! I've heard so much about her gallery."

And we had arrived.

So Hugh wasn't completely surprised by Patricia's warm welcome. Instead, it was I who was surprised, to find that Hugh had already selected two paintings from her gallery, both done by a local abstractionist, Ridley Goswell, who had lived in Naples for fifty years.

Goswell's work had become a staple for collectors who felt they had moved past an appreciation for realism and impressionism.

Although I did not care for Goswell's work, I knew many liked it. To me, it was suitable for use on textiles only; the designs were attractive but inscrutable as far as meaning goes.

I did not hold back when Hugh asked how I liked his choices: "Skillful but not meaningful to me. I prefer work that conveys a clear message, a thought I can receive and consider. That's why I like realism.

"I think Goswell's paintings convey only prettiness. I can see them as part of window drapes or upholstery. That does not, of course, mean they lack investment value. For that part, you should depend on Patricia's knowledge."

Hugh seemed disappointed, but Patricia took up her end of the conversation. "The market is full of varying opinions of abstract work because interpreting it remains so elusive. Much depends on the kind of effort that goes into a work. Has it texture? Does it include shapes? Layering? Does it convey a sense of movement? Does it give the viewer that thrill of experiencing beauty? Goswell's work, although partly geometric, does it for me. I think the elements in it are cohesive. I also detect some aspect of folk art."

That's where Hugh jumped in. "I see that, too. Folk art, I mean. As a person descended from Czechoslovakians, I look for the shapes in the weaving I grew up with. My grandmother was a weaver."

It turned out that Hugh's family name, Buranek, was Czech for "little ram." He was drawn to the kind of art he experienced as a child, art that included animal shapes as well as shapes from nature.

I began to look at the Goswell paintings in a new way. How could I have been so limiting? I had shut out a source of beauty because I had failed to understand it.

I thanked Patricia for her insights. Obviously, she was used to people being enlightened by her explanations. She asked her assistant to handle inquiries while she gave us tea in her office, continuing to talk about Ridley Goswell's work. Then she segued into a discussion of my own paintings and added, "You don't realize, Alice, how close some of your work cames to impressionism."

From a folder on her desk she extracted color prints of my Tree Series and showed them to Hugh. He professed to be delighted with them and asked if Patricia had any originals of mine to show. "Not at the moment; I've sold everything of hers that I had on my walls, but I know for a fact that Alice is working on something, although she won't tell me what it is."

Despite urging, I felt unable to discuss what I was painting, so in a few minutes Hugh and I left, Hugh thanking Patricia for her time and assuring her he would phone her soon.

In the car Hugh at first became silent. Finally, he inquired whether my reluctance to talk about my current work was his fault. He asked, "Is it because I like Ridley Goswell's work?"

"Not at all. I just feel possessive about my painting, and I think it's not yet ready to be examined. I must say that Patricia was very informative about Goswell, and I feel quite remiss in not having realized how interesting his work really is."

He took that as a peace offering, feeling free to speak more about his interest in Goswell's work.

We agreed to dine together at six with some new acquaintances of his at Locksley Glen, Caroline and Paul Benes, whom I knew only slightly.

That evening went smoothly. It seems that Benes, too, is a Czech name. Paul and Hugh compared notes about events in "the old country" while Caroline and I discussed Dr. Oz and the difficulty of finding comfortable shoes.

Despite general talk that centered on television news about volcano eruptions, earthquakes, mall murders, and campus rapes, I was able to return the conversation for a time to the beautiful art we had seen that day.

As I prepared to retire that evening, while I was painting my toenails with anti-fungal liquid and trying to recall whether I had already inserted my eye drops or sprayed my nostrils, I was jolted into remembering that I still needed to talk to Annabelle. The next morning I called to remind her she had agreed to dinner.

Annabelle came to the bar with a preoccupied demeanor. When she ordered V8 instead of a vodka martini, I knew she felt unable to relax. Too much was on her mind. When I asked how she was, the answer sounded strained: "I don't even know who I am any more."

"What do you mean, Annabelle?"

"I wonder if I'm my daughter's mother, or her kids' grandmother, or a woman who bossed ten employees in a home decorating business, or The Widow Ettling, or a guitar player, or Annabelle of Locksley Glen. Maybe none of the above."

"More likely, all of the above, Annabelle. Perhaps it's time to decide which role to emphasize. What would you like to do with the rest of your life? That's the question whose answer will help you decide the role you want to elevate. Or you could start from the opposite angle, by enumerating those roles you'd like to minimize."

"That's a good idea," she realized, sipping her juice. I passed her a bowl of popcorn, and almost immediately I could see her mind working. She came up with this decision: "I believe I'd like to see my daughter, and my grandchildren, about four times a year. Once a season. I'd rather visit my daughter's lovely home for a week at a time than have the family visit me here. That would keep my Florida life separate from my family life."

"Sounds sensible, Annabelle. What would your ideal Florida life include?"

"More music."

"You mean, more visits to the Naples Symphony?"

"Actually, more of my own music. I should practice so that I can occasionally give a program of guitar music here at the Glen. I studied classical guitar, which I love, for many years. Ever hear of a composer named Granados? He was my favorite. But I've neglected my music shamefully. Somehow, I thought it unsuited to my age and my life here. I know now that it isn't. I've finally realized there's nothing wrong with an old lady playing a guitar, if it's done well."

"Why Annabelle, that's wonderful! Hearing you play the guitar would enrich our lives as well as yours. You know how much we like it whenever Bill Hufferman sits down at the piano to deliver some tune we recognize. What else?"

"I should use my design knowledge. I've been noticing certain characteristics of the Florida style in furnishings. I think I could write a series of articles about them, adding my own ideas. I believe I could contribute something to this field, after all my years of experience. I'd explain what fits in and what doesn't, and why. I could call it 'the Florida Flavor.'"

"Wow, Annabelle! That's marvelous!" Heads turned my way after those exclamations, but I didn't care. I was genuinely thrilled for Annabelle. Of course, I wanted to believe that my probing questions had elicited these creative ideas for the Late Blooming of Annabelle Ettling. I realized, however, they must have been percolating in her mind for a long time.

Moreover, I began to see Annabelle in a new light: as a fellow member of the creative fraternity.

"I guess these ideas must have been in the back of my head for years," she admitted, underlining my own thought, "but you brought them out, and I'm grateful. Now if I can just follow through. . . ."

"You can, and you will, Annabelle. We'll all encourage you. For our sakes as well as yours."

I knew that following her new goals wouldn't be easy.

Annabelle had suffered from repeated urinary infections that left her feeling debilitated, but I believed firmly that because she now felt inspired to cultivate her creative side, she would overcome health obstacles like those infections and go on to become a productive person once more.

And a happier person.

During dinner. Annabelle talked of the letter she would write to her daughter about her decision. "As soon as she learns the reason for my not moving to Denver, she will understand. I need time alone here to improve my playing and to work out my design ideas."

"I'm sure of it, Annabelle. That sounds like a good strategy."

"I don't believe in stralogy, although I know my birth sign."

I smiled at her misunderstanding and continued encouraging her.

"As long as you yourself are convinced of the wisdom of your decision, you'll be able to help her realize how important your Florida life is to you."

"Alice One, you're a true friend. Thanks for helping me see what I knew already."

I basked in Annabelle's praise. And I thought her "stralogy" was clever. But I didn't stop wondering about the owner of the Wet Bathing Suit—and indeed, whether that owner was me, Alice One.

ELEVEN

While I was distracted by Hugh's art interests and Annabelle's problem, Locksley Glen held the monthly birthday dinner, for everyone whose birthday occurred in this month.

It wasn't my turn to attend, but I heard about it later from Katrina, who expected to learn a lot there. She was signing up for it when I emerged from the dining room after breakfast to look at the various signup sheets. I noticed that nobody had signed up for the trip to Bone Valley. Not even me. I guess we had already learned all we wanted to learn about the discoveries there.

At breakfast, Katrina had commented, "Just remembering the photos taken there is more than I want to know about it."

That was a side issue, anyway, I realized. Although our new understanding of that part of Florida was striking and hard to forget, it failed to assist us in figuring out whether the unidentified owner of the Wet Bathing Suit was alive or . . . not.

At that moment Katrina and her walker moved in behind me, and I turned, speaking my thoughts: "We still haven't learned whether the two people who are supposed to be on vacation are really there or. . . ."

". . . or are dead?"

"Don't say that, Katrina."

"Well, let's find out. This very minute. Surely Gordon Grambling is by now returned from gamboling in the islands, and Polly will be able to ask him to phone and check on those people. Along with any others supposed to be vacationing. The last I looked, it's September already. There's no longer much need to escape to the North from Florida's summer humidity."

I nodded, and we started for the front desk. Katrina's foot clumped along in the Big Black Cast. Then I stopped entirely.

"What's the matter?"

"I haven't seen Helene lately. Have you?"

"No, I haven't. Maybe she's unwell. I should call her. When I last talked to her, she was telling me that she had a new idea for her Halloween costume this year. Maybe she's been working on that."

"Okay, after we see Mr. Grambling we'll find out about Helene."

And we started off again. At the front desk Katrina asked Kelley Conners if we could see Mr. Grambling. We like to give him the courtesy of the title "Mr." or even "Director" because of his position. His face always beams when we play up his status. Making people happy takes so little.

"Mr. Grambling's office is being painted today," Kelley reported. "He's spending the day outside with Jimmy, checking on the work done by the new groundskeeping company we contracted with a couple of months ago. We haven't been entirely satisfied with their work," Kelley added, making herself part of the administration by the use of that "royal we." Even the cleaning women at Locksley Glen think of themselves as people who help run the place—as they do, of course.

"Jimmy" meant James DiParisi, the head of the Department of Environmental Services, who with his helpers was responsible for keeping everything at Locksley Glen in running order. Once he went so far as to replace my air conditioning system when it inexplicably stopped cooling my apartment on the year's hottest day.

Usually, however, the helpers' work consisted of less complicated tasks. They replaced burned-out ceiling light bulbs, they loosened blocked plumbing, and they took care of any box that arrived bearing the dreaded label, "Some Assembly Required." Since our range of physical abilities had been compromised, their ability to handle those everyday jobs made them invaluable to us.

At Kelley's announcement of the Director's schedule, Katrina and I looked at each other in disappointment. Naturally, we expected everybody in the administration to be ready to see us whenever we happened to want to talk to them. We had, however, discovered (although slowly) that life just doesn't work that way. So Katrina thanked Kelley, and we considered what to do next. We forgot momentarily about Helene.

"Why not go to see Polly and learn whether Marge O'Doul and . . . what's-her-name . . . are back from their trips?" Oh, lord, I forgot her name, I said to myself. "In fact," I added, "we should have done that before going to the director's office." I added that last point in an attempt to direct Katrina's attention away from the fact that the jeweler's name had unaccountably disappeared from my mind. I hate it when I forget a name.

"You mean Hermione Kreutzer," Katrina replied triumphantly. The name of the woman who made jewelry had leapt promptly from Katrina's brain to her tongue, and she pronounced it slowly for me, savoring her performance.

"Yes." Annoyed that Katrina's memory had dredged up Hermione's name faster than mine did, I refused to acknowledge her accomplishment and marched ahead of her toward Polly's office.

After all, that's the only time this week that I forgot a name. Well, the first time this week.

"Gotcha," I heard her say softly, but I pretended that my hearing had suddenly failed. Katrina has a habit of pointing out the obvious. And she's still doing it.

Polly, at least, sat at her desk, ready to accept all interruptions. She seemed curious about our second query concerning the vacationers, which showed our continuous concern, but we held back any explanation as we inquired about Marge and Hermione. Polly checked her records and reported, "Marge is due home tomorrow. Hermione, September 15."

We thanked her and left before any blinking started.

I announced to Katrina that since we were blocked from settling these matters, I was going to work on my painting. But Katrina did not let me depart. "You know, there's something we're forgetting," she said. "Maybe the bathing suit we saw in the Lost and Found box wasn't made by Boardwalk Beachwear, Astrid's company, but that doesn't mean it's not Astrid's suit. Perhaps it's hers after all. She could have patronized a company different from the one she worked for."

"Huh," I remarked profoundly. "I guess you're right. I think nobody has actually asked her about the suit." I stopped short of volunteering to track down Astrid and question her about her swim suit. I shrink from interrogating anyone who isn't a close friend about her or his personal habits. Besides, I was eager to get back to my painting. My sketches of Starr's leg had proved helpful, and to utilize them I had blocked in a corner of the painting that I was anxious to complete.

Katrina realized that I was unenthusiastic about the prospect of inquiring into what I saw as Astrid's personal life, so she graciously, or maybe ungraciously, took on the job herself. At the time, I didn't know that Katrina had a shortcut to this task already in mind, one that she believed might clarify Astrid's role in the matter, if any.

So we left each other, my reminding her that I would not be in the bar or dining room later, since I had accepted a dinner invitation from my friends Joe and Beth Arpeggio, residents of Beauty Bridge, the Naples senior community where I had lived for ten years in a cottage with my late husband Tim.

I enjoy renewing my friendship with the Arpeggios, although when I first decided to move to Locksley Glen, Joe and Beth questioned my decision. They thought that I had sentenced myself to occupy a cell in the Naples jail. But by now they realized that I loved my new home at Locksley Glen and was happy that I had moved there.

I looked forward to learning the news of Beauty Bridge from the Arpeggios. As I walked back to my apartment, I thought about the name of that community. It was certainly beauteous, but where was the bridge?

Suddenly I knew. The community itself was the bridge. Its residents were using it as the passageway to The Great Beyond.

TWELVE

L ocksley Glen held many parties, its activities director taking advantage of every holiday except National Diaper Day to schedule some fun.

Nobody cared to admit to wearing adult diapers, so we ordered them on the quiet, by the gross, in unmarked brown paper packages, as if they were pornographic films. Or maybe *with* pornographic films.

Residents celebrated every other possible occasion with a cocktail party involving special drinks and a themed dinner, afterwards enjoying the music of Larry Lopat's Orchestra. These parties took place amid balloons, streamers, banners, and large fake flowers or other symbolic objects mounted in the Living Room by our activities director, Brett Bozeman.

At the time of the Jewish New Year, which occurred near the end of September, people with names like O'Malley and McPhail celebrated to klezmer music as heartily as did people called Edelstein and Gorsky. On St. Patrick's Day, when even the vodka was green... no, I think I won't tell that story.

On these occasions some residents ventured onto the dance floor, although not for long, because painful legs and lapses in ability to move soon set in. Pain caused the would-be dancers to hobble to their seats, wondering why they had tried to act young. They compensated by ordering another Margarita, forgetting that they had already downed two.

One of the parties everyone enjoyed was the monthly birthday party, an affair which residents with a birthday in that month were invited to share. For these residents, Locksley Glen held a private dinner in the Large Game Room. Birthday dinners were fancier than usual, going so far as to offer champagne and lavishly sauced lobster tails as well as birthday cake so rich as to cause our many diabetics and our celiac sufferers no end of digestive difficulty.

A resident celebrating a birthday in a particular month was allowed to bring to this party one guest, who had to be a resident and could be a spouse or even a friend. Katrina, I knew, was attending this month, although she was not celebrating her own birthday. Her BFF, Bill Hufferman, whose birth month was September, had invited her. And that was where she planned to speak to Astrid.

Katrina had discovered, through the list printed in our monthly newsletter, that Astrid, like Bill, was one of the September birthday kids, and Katrina had plotted an approach she believed would put a final answer to our question about Astrid's swimsuits. She planned to corner Astrid and prevent an escape until she had received a satisfactory answer to the question: was Astrid the one who left her bathing suit at the pool?

Kidlike behavior is the rule at these parties. Silly hats and volunteered songs always make the birthday celebrants feel like children again. The champagne and the general atmosphere of hilarity help residents temporarily forget their pains and the other physical limitations that inconvenience them. Katrina planned to take advantage of the relaxed attitude this party engendered to find out if Astrid was the owner of the black bathing suit.

As Katrina told the story later, on their arrival at the party she and Bill scanned the room for Astrid, but they were too early. She hadn't shown up yet. They hung out for a while at the champagne table, standing there sipping longer than they really wanted to. But soon she entered, a tall, quiet figure in a neat white dress decorated in European peasant style with blue cross-stitches and smocking.

Katrina, with her European bent, particularly appreciated the style dress that Astrid had chosen. She immediately decided to use the dress as the opening for her conversation with Astrid about bathing suits.

Approaching Astrid, Katrina suddenly noticed that Aidan, one of the Birthday Boys of the month, was about to "shanghai the quarry," as she put it. She saw that he intended to be seated next to Astrid. He quickly asked her to join him at Table Seven, where three residents already sat. "I like tall women," he announced as he led her there by the elbow.

Katrina noticed with distaste that Astrid passively accepted Aidan's hands-on steering. She and Bill had no choice but to follow and fill in the open seats.

Before Katrina could launch her opening gambit, Aidan, ignoring Katrina and Bill, was already talking to Astrid about Norway, where it seems he had once visited. Although Astrid replied in monosyllables ("Uh, yes" and "Uh, no"), Aidan held forth on the Vikings, the German invasion of 1940, and a fjord he once saw that boasted four waterfalls.

Then Aidan asked, "How is your husband today?" Katrina, learning from their conversation that Anders had been hospitalized with congestive heart failure, realized that Aidan must have planned this "date" with Astrid. She decided not to permit him to dominate the conversation.

As Katrina told it, Bill engaged the others at the table— our friend Bob Avery, a man named Hugh, and our recent acquaintance Shelley Pace—while she interjected a question about Astrid's experience as a bathing suit model in California. She timed it when Aidan had just been served a shrimp cocktail that was impossible to eat without using the fingers and without smearing red cocktail sauce on the face.

The three giant shrimp in each serving perched precariously on the side of a little bowl of cocktail sauce instead of resting on a flat surface, so they could not be sliced. They had to be grabbed by the tail and eaten out of hand. Dripping, splashing, and smearing were inevitable. Talking was delayed.

Katrina ignored her appetizer in order to talk to Astrid and finally reached the point of asking whether she owned a black two-piece bathing suit like the one now in the Lost and Found box.

"I don't know," Astrid replied. "I have several black suits," she added vaguely. Before Katrina could continue, Aidan jumped in with flirtatious remarks about wanting to see Astrid in a bathing suit, asking her to swim with him the next morning, and inquiring as to what suit she might wear. Astrid became even less committal. Katrina's view of twin splashes of cocktail sauce on Aidan's cheeks especially irritated her.

No doubt, Katrina thought, Astrid's lack of conversation meant that she was worried about her husband. Perhaps, as a married woman, she was also surprised at being pursued so assiduously by Aidan.

Katrina then became aware of Shelley Pace's interest in the Aidan-Astrid exchanges. Shelley's face had become the very essence of disappointment. Obviously, she had hoped for attention from Aidan, and her hopes had been dashed. Bob Avery seemed to be acting kindly toward Shelley, but he, too, revealed by his glances that he was interested in talking to Astrid, now that she was appearing in public without her husband.

Bob began interjecting himself into the conversation and talked about Norwegian music, even though Grieg seemed to be the only composer he could think of. Once he made a mistake and mentioned Smetana, but Astrid turned to him with a surprised look. She knew Smetana was a Czech.

Katrina felt frustrated. Because she found Astrid continuing to be vague about her swimming attire, she eventually gave up on trying to pin the woman down to anything. She turned to Bill, who was talking to Hugh.

Bill discovered that this man must be Football Hugh of the thick eyebrows, whom I had mentioned meeting at breakfast one day, and began a conversation with him about the National Football League. Katrina joined Bill and Hugh in sharing opinions about their favorite teams.

Katrina discovered that Hugh knew more than football. "I asked whether he had any other interests, and he surprised me by talking about art," Katrina told me later. "He mentioned that he had recently met a woman named Alice who was later revealed to be an artist. He wondered how to get in touch with her, since he dabbled in art himself. I gave him your last name so that he could use the Residents' List to phone you," she related to me with a smile.

"So you're the one who did it. Well, it turned out okay. We visited Patricia Knightsbridge's gallery together and talked about art." I was also thinking: it's nice that somebody wants to talk to me. Maybe not with me exactly, but with somebody who can talk about art.

THIRTEEN

Later that day, Starr suddenly came up with what we both considered the travel deal of the decade. "Listen, Alice One," she said on the phone. "Have you ever done a private tour of San Francisco, including Chinatown and the Asian Art Museum? Well, two places are left in a five-day guided tour by a historian from Keio University in Japan who is a specialist in Oriental enclaves in American cities. Two people got sick and dropped out, and there's no time to conduct the usual advertising because we leave next Monday. The company has cut the prices for these last two places. I'm taking one of them; do you want the other?"

I've always wanted to experience the Orient and have never been there, so I figured this would be the closest I would ever get to it, at my advanced age. I couldn't resist the offer. I dropped my work, read all the printed information about the tour, which sounded fascinating, paid the fee in advance, and coordinated with Starr on how to join the tour.

For us, it would begin in Miami with a direct flight to San Francisco. There, we were booked at a hotel for one night in order to meet the other tour members and our guide. I even persuaded Starr to let me include her name in my memo to

Polly explaining when (and where) I would be away from Locksley Glen. This time, Starr wouldn't need her aide to cover for her absence.

As for luggage, we were advised to bring only one piece, an overnighter or weekender that we could lift with one hand because we were going to be touring the city on a small van and staying at various hotels. Each evening, we would get off the van, carry our own bags into a restaurant, have dinner, then carry the bags to a hotel that is either nearby or in the same building as the restaurant. As a result, I wore the same suit all week, just changing blouses and underclothes, which I rinsed out at each hotel. Drip dries proved essential for this trip.

The other members of our party surprised me. Most of them were academics or technicians. A Chinese-Canadian couple from Vancouver, Canada, consisted of two sociologists. The two Japanese-Americans from Portland, Oregon—also a couple—were both software engineers. An Italian-American woman from Denver designed purses and luggage for a firm in Italy. Two blond male biologists from Philadelphia with Germanic names worked for a forensics lab.

We were a mixed bag. And we had little opportunity to talk, so we approached the problem of getting along by smiling a lot. Of course, Starr and I were obviously much older than the others, but they politely said nothing about our status as Travelers Who Were Old.

The tour leader was Dr. Kano, a scholarly-looking woman of about forty. Not only was she a Keio University graduate, she had also worked for the Asahi newspaper, which I knew was a huge empire with many interests. Two years ago she had moved to San Francisco to start her travel business and had since become an American citizen.

Dr. Kano, a diminutive powerhouse, never seemed to rest. After a day packed with lecturing and leading us around, she joined us at dinner, where she ate little and answered a lot of questions. She would then finish with a preview of the following day's delights. She was always ready to depart again at 8:30 A.M. The driver, Alphonse, was a Caucasian of French origin, and she often spoke to him in his own language. Dr. Kano was an impressive woman.

We found the tour well-organized, with every day carefully planned and tightly scheduled, but there was always a stop for lunch, and occasionally we had an hour's free time. Once Starr proposed to me that during a free hour she and I take a taxi to tour the Vibrator Museum, but my mortified look in response to that suggestion made her withdraw the idea. I had to assure her that I knew what a vibrator was before she would stop suggesting that we "hop in a cab and check it out."

I guess Starr is more liberated than I am. The idea of visiting a public museum devoted to such a private object as a vibrator made me shrink into my seat with embarrassment. Instead, Starr agreed to join me in shopping at a department store, and I bought a few Christmas presents for my Cleveland relatives.

I found the San Francisco tour enlightening, especially seeing Chinatown—and even Japan-town—with the aid of Dr. Kano's commentary. The Asian Art Museum was almost overwhelming in its beauty; I'm so glad I had the privilege of viewing it. I'd never seen so many gorgeous Buddhas in my life.

For fun I liked Fisherman's Wharf best. The huge male sea otters pushing younger ones off the floats made me think of the human business world, where status is so important and leads to much jockeying for position. For stunning views, I loved seeing the vista that included the graceful-looking Golden Gate Bridge just as our little van turned left into Golden Gate Park, with the impressive Presidio ahead.

Actually, I think the trip was a little too much for me, at my age. Touring required considerable walking, standing, and utilizing painful knees to get on and off the van. I had to take pain pills often because of my old, worn-out bones and stiff back. Starr seemed to weather it well, but I did see her using her inhaler several times.

Near the end of the trip I actually contemplated withdrawing from the tour but decided to stick it out, determined that if Starr could do it, so could I. She teased me by claiming that we should have gone to That Special Museum so that we would have something about which to make private jokes. When I got back to my apartment in Naples, I fell into bed, exhausted, and slept for ten hours.

As for progress in the case of the Wet Bathing Suit during our absence, Starr and I detected none. I found my mind distracted from the problem by my stimulating experiences on the West Coast. I had even made several sketches of gorgeous objects in the Asian Art Museum, like the symbols called mandalas, and wanted time to think about them. I decided that I might be inspired to produce something with an Oriental influence.

Several email messages—one from Patricia Knightsbridge—and phone messages awaited my attention, as a little red flashing light on my studio answering machine kept reminding me, and I needed to collect my snailmail. Catching up would take a while.

Moreover, we had made friends among some of the other tourists and wanted to keep in touch with them. Starr had been drawn to the Denver purse and luggage designer, and the two of them had enjoyed talking fashion and travel. They were considering how they might collaborate on some project.

I had exchanged ideas and business cards with the two young sociologists from British Columbia, who found themselves curious about the issue of housing for the elderly, a problem they realized that Starr and I had solved to our satisfaction. They were considering a formal study of the topic. I was sure I could be of help to them in enumerating various aspects of the problem that people my age face when thinking of how to spend the last years of their lives.

How refreshing it was to find that our ideas, although they came from old people, seemed welcome to younger ones!

Life is full! I thought. There's so much to do.... But in the back of my mind there remained that nagging question: Had a crime been committed here at Locksley Glen? And would we ever find out?

FOURTEEN

"I hate September," Helene growled. "I see this month as a cloaked man coming to steal away the sun. Both my husbands died in September, almost exactly 20 years apart. And now I'm weakening so much. Can hardly walk. Need to be helped on and off the toilet. Can't see, can't hear. Can't read. Can't even decipher my own writing. Don't want to live like this." And she turned her head away from us.

It was Barbara Boobs who learned that Helene was holed up in her apartment refusing to get out of bed and suffering from depression. Barbara had thought to interview Helene for the next sketch of a resident to appear in the Glen's newsletter, but Helene had demurred.

Nurse Noonan assured us that Helene's family in New Jersey had been informed of her situation and that one of her sons was flying in on the weekend to talk to his mother.

I was shocked to hear Helene use the metaphor of a cloaked man, the same one I had recently conjured up in a scary vision. Perhaps, I thought, this figure was a phenomenon common among old people. When I mentioned it later to Katrina, she responded, "Actually, it's a common enough vision even among children. It appears to represent the dark side of one's personality. Some analysts think we all have a dark side."

That was hardly a soothing insight, because I was beginning to realize that I might have one, too.

Three of us sat there in Helene's bedroom trying to think of something to say to her. The reason we found it hard to think of a suitable way to start is that we ourselves often needed some reassurance that life was worth living in our eighties and nineties. Our confidence that we had a future in this life had been undermined by experiences during which we, as old people, suddenly became invisible when we were part of social groups that included young, active people.

We old people often feel that we have become background to the young. Part of the landscape. We feel like observers, not participants, when we become aware that nobody wants our opinions. Who wants to talk to someone who isn't fully engaged in the life of today and who may know only about the past? Not most young people.

Of course, some seniors feed the stereotype by refusing to enter the computer age. To them "social media" means the Clubs Column of the local newspaper. A spotty embrace of the latest in modern life indicates to young people that we know nothing.

We are all familiar with what it feels like to have nobody address us or ask us about ourselves because of assumptions about the elderly that might or might not be accurate. There have been times when I wanted to shout, "Old people are not obsolete! We still have something to contribute!"

No wonder we often prefer the company of people our own age.

Katrina, as usual, found the words we all required for this occasion. "Helene, we need you in our little group of friends. We're looking for help in figuring out what's happening here. We need your opinions. Who but you will be outspoken enough to say what we are all thinking? Who but you can cut through the hype and put it to us in plain vanilla, undecorated with any chocolate sprinkles? Who but you do we all love and respect? Please let your aide dress you, and join us for dinner. We need you."

"Hurry up and get with the program, Helene," added Joan. "We require your ideas on what is going on here. We're worried that the Wet Bathing Suit is a clue that something serious might have happened. Marge O'Doul has returned from Boston, but Hermione Kreutzer is missing."

Joan's words, following on Katrina's persuasion, had the desired effect, and eventually Helene muttered, "Okay. Only for you."

"Thank you, Helene," I responded. "We'll be waiting in the bar at six." Relieved, I deposited on a bedside table the little potted plant I had carried in and said, "We brought you a gift, but you'll have to take care of it. It won't live unless you do." A grunt of disapproval was our only answer, but we received it gladly.

In the Living Room we settled ourselves at a large table in the corner farthest from the bar, where we were unlikely to be overheard as we made plans to review what we knew, and lacked knowledge of, concerning the Wet Bathing Suit.

Gathered at the big round table were Joan and Clarence, the only married couple; Bill and Katrina, who were close friends and perhaps more than that; Lucas of the white hair and grandfatherly manner; Annabelle, recently renewed in spirit; Starr, our elegant and sophisticated ex-travel agent; Ed Champion of the Kentucky Colonel accent, who this time showed up in a cervical collar around his neck; and me. That made nine, and Helene would be ten.

We delegated Lucas to negotiate with Thalia, the Dining Room supervisor, for use at 7:00 of the Private Dining Room, a small version of the regular one, because it seats a maximum of twelve people who can talk together more privately than in the main room.

Some residents interested in the problem that consumed us weren't present: Alice Two was having dinner at Mount Vesuvius Restaurant with a long-time Naples friend who resided in the condo where Alice had once lived. Joyce Joslin was at Happy Hearts Rehab, getting therapy for her heart condition. Bob Avery hadn't responded to phone messages left for him.

Mary Two had called Katrina to say she'd had a trying day, wasn't feeling up to coming to the Dining Room, and would order a dinner tray. We all knew she was contemplating a hip replacement her surgeon had recommended and that she found the prospect daunting. Who wouldn't?

That kind of operation puts old people out of commission for what seems like a long time, during which they must rely on the assistance of others in order to recover from the procedure, accepting help with the most private functions of daily living. Then, forsaking all other activities, they must work diligently at rehabilitation to regain their former abilities, such as they are. Committing to an operation means shutting just about everything else out of one's life.

We were chatting about Mary Two's predicament when Laurette, Helene's daytime private-duty aide, rolled our friend into the room in her deluxe wheelchair complete with rubber tires, rear-view mirror, and a 1930s Ooga Horn. Helene had roused herself for us. She looked regal but pale, and we winced at seeing the dark crescents under her eyes. She wore a bright yellow quilted jacket. A lacy white lap rug covered her infected knee.

Laurette grinned with pleasure and exclaimed cheerfully to herself in Haitian French as she skillfully maneuvered the wheelchair around empty seats and abandoned walkers, evidently scolding those objects for blocking her path. She rolled her charge triumphantly to the spot we had reserved for Helene at the barroom table, announced in English that she would return in thirty minutes, and left.

Ed Champion, ever the Southern gentleman, sprang to his feet, or tried to spring—it turned out to be more of a sideways froglike lurch—and gave Helene what passed for a bow of welcome, calling out "Madame Helene! What a pleash-ouahhhh," putting as much of a Kentucky spin on the words as he could muster. His neck brace made him look more like a turtle than a frog, especially when he bent down to massage his knees, which had been affected the most by his sudden and ill-advised leap.

"Sit down," Helene replied in her usual bored tone. "Are you suffering from whiplash? Or St. Vitus Dance?"

That last illness is one we hadn't heard named since childhood. I think by now it must have an entirely new identity. It's probably illegal these days to name an illness after a saint.

Ed explained in standard Midwestern English, "I have a chronic spinal cord condition that sometimes requires the use of a cervical collar."

"Hmm. Well, let's get on with it." Having passed inspection, Ed sat down. The rest of us made squeals of delight at seeing our friend dressed and out of bed. Joan even tried to take Helene's hand, but it was quickly extracted. This was our down-to-earth, businesslike Helene. "Will somebody get me a gin and tonic?"

Helene had obviously decided to ignore the rule forbidding alcohol while taking drugs. Doubtless, she had decided she was above such warnings. Or she was thinking, as I've heard others say aloud, "How could it matter, this late in my life?"

Lucas volunteered before anyone else could, and while he was gone, Helene had to put up with greetings from other well-wishers who came over, despite our effort at privacy, and stopped to say "hello" and "welcome back." These were people like Barbara Boobs, and also a ninety-nine-year-old woman named Minnie, who used a gold cane that matched her bracelet and necklace. A fragile-looking man called Dinsmore riding a self-propelled chair rose, unpredictably, from his machine and tried to give her a kiss but nearly tipped over onto her. She held him at bay with one hand at his chest, and he finally subsided. "Go away, Dinsmore!" she commanded. "You're acting foolish."

At length (and it seemed extremely long), Lucas appeared with the requested drink. Helene carefully used both hands to take a few sips. Finally, after shaking her head at a popcorn bowl proffered by Joan and setting down her drink, Helene got right to the point. "So what do you know about this Wet Bathing Suit that was left at the pool? And why do you suspect foul play?"

For some reason we looked at Katrina, so she began.

FIFTEEN

"Helene," Katrina began, "we can't get any response from our many requests that someone identify the owner of the suit. We even had the director print a notice in the GleNewsletter. We know the person who owned the suit was a resident because no guests were staying here during the week it was left at the pool, so we wonder why someone who owns a perfectly nice two-piece suit like that is refusing to claim it.

"Could it be simply from embarrassment at having taken it off? Or could she have been forced to take it off by some sexual predator and become so traumatized by her experience that she was afraid to admit it was hers? Could she even have... been unable to claim it? Murder, although unexpected, is not unheard of in Naples, Florida."

"Murder? At Locksley Glen?"

Just then we were interrupted by having Joan sit up straight and open her eyes wide. She sat facing the door, so we all turned toward it and craned our necks in an attempt to see the person she had spotted approaching us. It was Bob Avery, his hair more unruly than ever. His face showed one very black eye and a large forehead bruise in an exotic shade that an artist would identify readily as Persian Purple. "What happened?" Joan inquired.

"Don't ask," he replied. "My life is no longer an open bush." And he walked directly to the bar, calling for a double Scotch without even waiting to see if we had noticed his borrowing of Annabelle's phrase. It was clear to us that he was so wrapped up in what had happened to him that he felt unable to participate.

Katrina couldn't resist recalling an earlier conversation: "Maybe Bob is finally suffering from FOGO." Some of us remembered and smiled. The man in question either failed to hear the remark or chose not to hear it, because he didn't reply.

"Does he look injured?" Helene asked. We'd forgotten her poor eyesight.

"Black eye and forehead bruise," replied Ed.

"Fell in the bathroom," Helene explained. "Typical injuries. Probably has more bruises, covered by his clothing. Now, about the bathing suit. Has any resident shown any particular interest in bathing suits?"

We looked at Katrina. She knew, and we knew she knew. "Yes," she admitted, "a resident named Aidan MacCracken. He's been trying to date a woman named Astrid, who was once a bathing suit model, ever since he met her at the monthly Birthday Dinner. Even though she is married. Her husband is in the hospital.

"Aidan has been attending the swimming exercises just to watch, as well as going to the beach parties admittedly in the hope of seeing us in our swimwear."

"He must be a bathing suit freak," inserted Annabelle. Bob stirred uncomfortably in his chair at the bar. He'd heard that one.

"That's not a foregone conclusion," scolded Helene. "Is there any other evidence? Looking avidly at half-naked women is pretty normal. Does anyone think him capable of violence?"

At first nobody said anything. Then, rather reluctantly, I said, "He no longer greets me, and he's given me angry looks since I refused to paint his dead wife from photos."

"Angry looks?" Helene nodded. "I have always distributed those widely myself. It's merely a sign of being touchy and self-centered. Anything else?"

A sudden announcement interrupted our discussion. "The Private Dining Room is ready," said the server named Jose, who walked more quietly than our weakened hearing had detected. So we obeyed the summons and paraded past the Main Dining Room toward the smaller one next door, Laurette steering Helene's chariot. Bob remained at the bar.

In the hallway I passed Paul and Caroline Benes, along with Hugh, and they all smiled and nodded at me. Hugh waved.

"Why is that man waving? Is he giving directions?" Helene remarked with disapproval.

"He just knows me, Helene. We talk about art." And our march into the small room continued. We seated ourselves so that Helene would rule at the head.

"You talk about art. Good. Anything else?"

"Not really."

"You mean not yet."

Snickers all around, at my expense. I was glad to finally be seated. Embarrassed, I raised my menu to my face. Of course, that helped me read it, too. Restaurant menus, including those at Locksley Glen, are all printed in such small type that, without a portable magnifying glass, one could miss the entire first course before getting the print deciphered.

"Tell me again about the people who are missing," Helene began.

Clarence replied, "Only one now, the jewelry designer Hermione Kreutzer. She spends a couple of months each summer with her son's family in Virginia. She was due back last week, but she hasn't arrived, and nobody is answering her family's phone."

"Obviously, they've decided to drive her back here," Helene surmised.

"Yeah, that makes sense," said Clarence.

"But we've discovered, Helene, that it's possible to leave here for an extended time without announcing one's absence to the administration in advance, so maybe someone else is absent," I contributed.

"I doubt it," said Starr.

Amazed, I began, "But, Starr…"

"I know. I did it. I left for nearly a week, and nobody in the administration found out. But I discovered later that the aide who helps me with my baths knew I was away and covered for me, even though I didn't ask her to. I know why: she sometimes gets the same kind of hankering I do," she added with a sly smile and a wink.

"Hmph" is all I could answer. I guess that wink means Starr thinks I'm a stodgy old codger who wouldn't consider slipping around a rule, even if an aide would cover for me.

She's probably right.

And then the server, Jose, began taking our ten dinner orders, so we were reduced to relative silence for about five minutes.

When that was over, Helene handed down the opinion that we were probably concerned for no reason and about nothing. "The discarded suit doubtless has a logical explanation, although it eludes me."

Then Lucas came up with something else: "I heard a rumor yesterday that Aidan was leaving Locksley Glen."

"Maybe he's going to join a boy band," quipped Bill.

"Actually, he is said to have plans for entering an assisted living residence in Tampa."

"He's unhappy here?" I asked.

"I guess."

"Well, some of us are unhappy with him."

"Who said that?" Helene asked.

Wishing I could shrink below my seat, I volunteered, "I did. Alice One."

"Why do you say that, Alice One?"

"Because of the malevolent glances he gives me since I refused to paint his dead wife from photos. I also responded indignantly to his false assumptions about the nature of painting. He tried to denigrate my entire career."

I'm afraid I sounded a bit petulant.

"So you prefer the hand-waving of the man who saw you come in with us?"

Everyone laughed but me. "Why not? At least it's not negative, and it's based on an informed opinion."

"Good for you, Alice One. You've got spunk. So you see this person, Aidan, as negative and uninformed. Does that make him a likely suspect as a rapist or murderer?"

"No, but it does make him unlikeable." I suppose I was pouting—a word my mother used for me much too often. I began to wonder why my childhood memories kept intruding on the present.

"You expect to like everyone, then, and look askance at those who fail to live up to your expectations."

"Of course. Living cheek by jowl in this building with a hundred people almost demands that one try to be likeable. Of course, I am alone in my apartment a lot, in order to do my work, but not all the time. I also need to mix with people in the common rooms, so that means I have to try to be polite.

"I think all of us should try to be courteous to others, so that we can get along. If someone fails to try, he or she becomes suspect. Why come here at all, if you don't want to fit in?"

"Admirable sentiments indeed, although demonstrating a defensive attitude. But I doubt strongly that we are dealing here with a criminal. Probably just a narcissist."

"Then why are we so worried that there is a body that's missing from inside that bathing suit? And whose is it?"

Rustles, clicks, and clacks approached: salads and soups were being served by Jose, with the help of Maria, his assistant of the day. Helene was granted a reprieve, so we attacked our food. Acting like detectives is hungry work. Yet nothing had been settled. After dinner, Helene was too tired to talk any more. Laurette came in and whisked her away. Her departure was followed by murmurings of disappointment.

So we were back where we started.

That evening Hugh called, asking me to join him and his friends in the Dining Room the following evening and tell about my San Francisco trip. Curiously, this dinner brought us a new idea that eventually helped us find the answer to our questions.

SIXTEEN

As it happened, Caroline Benes was hospitalized that morning; she had suffered a T.I.A., a minor stroke. At Locksley Glen, something was always happening to somebody. Although Caroline was expected to make a complete recovery, her rehabilitation would take a while. I wouldn't be seeing her soon to talk about shoes... or Dr. Oz.

I liked her, although I disapproved of the tight sweaters she wore. But I realized that all of us were used to dressing in a particular way and seldom altered it as we aged, even if it became less appropriate.

Caroline's husband Paul, after spending the afternoon with her in the hospital, joined Hugh and me at dinner. The presence of two men at my table made me the subject of heavy teasing by women friends entering the Dining Room: "Alice One! Dining with *two men*? What are you trying to do, corner the market? Leave some for the rest of us!" And more of the same.

When Katrina came by with a similar thrust, I parried it by asserting, with a grin, that I had invited her boyfriend, Bill, as well, and that he planned to desert her and join us.

That stopped her.

Hugh had entered the Dining Room limping and leaning on Paul's arm, but I decided not to mention his condition in case he was sensitive about sharing the cause. I remembered Bob's reaction to our query about his injuries. Maybe, I thought, in Annabelle's words, Hugh's life isn't an open bush.

Hugh opened the art conversation by saying that, although he loved art, during his only visit to San Francisco he had toured the Museum of Science rather than the Oriental Art Museum. He wanted me to describe some of the art exhibits.

His friend Paul, obviously worried about his wife, squirmed in his seat. He played with his food, made some pretense of listening, and jumped when his cellphone rang—a stepson was calling. Paul left us early to return to his apartment and talk to Caroline on his land line, keeping the cell free for incoming family calls.

Hugh, I learned, was being nagged by pain just like the rest of us. Sometimes, what seems like a minor problem can deliver as much discomfort as a major illness. He was taking pain pills for an ingrown toenail that had just undergone aggressive treatment at his podiatrist's office. The pills and the loose sandals he was wearing hadn't done much for his raw toe, and he was grateful to be distracted by hearing about the art museum.

Between the salads and the main entrees, I described what for me was the museum's dominating feature: room after room full of gorgeous carved or cast Buddhas representing several different cultural and religious traditions. Many of the statues gleamed with gold.

As I munched my broccoli, I realized that hearing about statues of Buddha left Hugh cold; he was responding only with "humph" and "oh." I would have to think of some other aspect of the museum that he might find curious and attractive.

"Have you ever examined mandalas?" I ventured. "The museum features a lot of these, since they're part of the spiritual tradition of the East."

"No, what are they?"

"They're circles with intricate designs. Mandalas are round, but the designs inside them are based on a square, so they're geometric. I think they must be designed on graph paper, or perhaps with the aid of a protractor. Or both.

"In many of them I detected designs that resembled petals. Most are black-and-white, so at a distance they convey the impression of lace, or the face of a large, round flower. In other words, they're beautiful."

"Why are they part of a spiritual tradition?" Hugh lowered his chin and looked at me through his heavy eyebrows, but this time I knew he wasn't threatening; he was just intensely curious.

"They're used in meditation, an activity that's been spreading from East to West for nearly a century."

"I know. My daughter says she meditates every morning for twenty minutes, and she believes it helps her stay away from cigarettes."

"I've never heard about that use of meditation, but it makes sense."

"Where do mandalas fit into this?"

"Ready for dessert?" interrupted our server, Maurizio. I passed, but Hugh asked for the carrot cake.

I went on about mandalas. I guess I was "warming to my subject," as writers say, perhaps because Hugh showed real interest, one that coincided with mine.

"I've read about using a mandala for meditation, and I may try it out, since I can't seem to meditate in any other way. I understand that meditating has great health benefits.

"To use a mandala, first you decide on what is called your "intention" — that is, what you want to do. Use of the mandala is supposed to help you overcome any blocks to reaching your goal.

"You do this by clearing your mind of everything else and concentrating all your attention on the mandala. You let its design encompass you—try to immerse yourself in it mentally, the way you do with thrilling music. Supposedly, you will eventually be enlightened—that is, you will become aware of a clear path to your goal."

"Sounds curious but possible."

"I mean to try it, but not before attempting to make my own mandalas. That might be the most fun of all—just designing the symbols."

Hugh leaned forward. "So a new art project is coming up. You haven't given up on your current painting, have you? I still hope to get a view of it when it's finished."

"I'm working on that, but this little project seems to be a way to experiment with something new, like a toy. I'm not sure how to begin, but I think I would need a protractor to create a mandala. I remember getting one of those little instruments for math in elementary school, but of course I don't have one now. I must have discarded mine long ago.

"Do you remember Erma Bombeck, the humorist?" She used to write a syndicated column. She once wrote that the average time between the day you throw something away and the day you want it back again is two weeks. I guess she was wrong; it can be as long as seventy years."

Hugh laughed at Erma's lament. I decided to ask about his interest in Ridley Goswell's work. "Speaking of geometric designs, have you made a decision about the paintings you were looking at in Patricia Knightsbridge's gallery?"

Nodding, he finished his cake and, straightening up, announced, "I've bought both of them and had them hung in my living room. I discovered that I especially like the row of symbols resembling trees on the left side of one painting, and the odd shapes that look like animals floating around in the other. Want to come up to my apartment and see how they fit in?

"I think I'm asking you, in time-honored fashion, if you'd like to see my etchings!"

It was my turn to laugh. "Thanks, but I can't this evening. I'm meeting a friend at 7:30 in the theatre. We want to see the new Chris Markel film, *Below the Rim*, and Brett Bozeman is showing it tonight."

"Another time, then."

I nodded, and we left. As usual, I had trouble rising from my chair because of my arthritic knees and ankles. He limped pitifully as he moved away from the table. What a pair! Commiserating, we parted.

As I returned to my apartment, I reflected on the ways we deal with pain. Much of the time, we pretend it isn't even there. Each day, whenever I pass a friend in the hall, I am greeted with "Good morning, Alice One. How are you?"

I answer in the usual way: "Fine, Katrina. How are you?" We lie a lot. I know Katrina's knees are giving her trouble, and she knows my spinal stenosis is nagging at me. But unless our pains are new and unusual, we don't bother mentioning them, because what good would it do? Nobody really wants to hear about our pain.

If our daily and regular aches and stabs have subsided for the moment, we still have mental distress to deal with. As I look around, I see a friend suffering because she has a dying daughter, another with a son who had a terrible accident, and one who has just lost her husband, her companion of sixty years. One has been told she has an incurable disease.

No wonder we all sometimes become touchy, grouchy, or withdrawn.

Aging is not for the timid (I told myself), so don't bother getting old unless you're tough enough to take it. That's not an original thought; it comes from the Locksley Glen hairdresser, who is approaching retirement age herself and, from what she's observed here, is steeling herself for the future.

SEVENTEEN

The next morning, as I left my apartment, I found a plastic bag hanging on my doorknob. Opening it, I lifted out a box that contained a protractor. Shades of fifth grade! The instrument resembled my elementary school instrument, and I was glad to have it. Going back inside, I sent a quick "thank you" email to Hugh, who had given me his internet address before I left him the evening before.

In the hall I met Polly, who told me that Hermione had finally returned, having been driven back to Locksley Glen by her family, since her son was concerned about the increasing neuropathy in her feet and legs. This condition made it difficult for her to board and dismount from a plane, to say nothing of her obviously dire need of a walker, something that is hard to use on aircraft. That's why he decided to drive her back to Naples and see that she got the help she needed. Helene was correct again: Hermione was no longer missing.

Breakfast with Starr, Katrina, and Bill, which I thought would present an opportunity to talk about mandalas and protractors, proved to be dreary. Katrina announced that Ed Champion, our would-be Kentuckian, had collapsed the evening before. An ambulance had taken him to the hospital to find out what was wrong.

Joan came over to our table to say that she and Clarence would be checking on Ed's progress. "We'll keep calling the hospital and bugging them till we find out whether he's been admitted. That's all they'll tell us because we're not family."

"He may be in the E.R. for hours, while they diagnose him," Katrina warned.

"I know. We'll both be at home all day today. Tomorrow will be different; Clarence goes in for an adjustment to the pacemaker for his heart."

"Ugh," said Katrina. "How's Helene?"

"Okay. I talked to her son. He's trying to persuade her to consider living in New York, either near him or with him and his family."

"I can't see Helene flourishing in New York," Katrina said.

"Not the city. Her son lives in a beautiful suburb, Chappaqua. The Clintons live there. Helene's son is retired, and his wife doesn't work outside the home. It might be a good place for our friend. She obviously needs constant care and distraction from her thoughts."

Katrina nodded reluctantly. "I see. I'll give her a call later today."

I could tell that I wouldn't get a chance to talk about mandalas, so when finished, I left.

There was one more interruption to my work that I had to deal with. The approach of Halloween, which was always celebrated in lively fashion at Locksley Glen, meant I had to think of a new costume idea.

Long-time residents like me were expected to display group spirit by taking part in every social event, if not in the hospital or confined to our apartments, and for Halloween I needed a costume.

I had been putting off working on this challenge, but with the mention of Helene, I'd recalled that before she became ill she had already thought of how she wanted to dress for the annual Locksley Glen Halloween Party. Some people spend months planning and preparing elaborate costumes for this occasion. Maybe Helene wouldn't actually get to the party this year, but I knew that I should, and it was time that I put my brain to work on this matter.

I could not help smiling as I recalled some of last year's costumes: Bob Avery as a convict in a striped onesie, Lucas as a pirate who couldn't recall the words of the jaunty song he was supposed to sing, Joan in her collapsing Marie Antoinette hairdo, Ed as a pregnant German bar-room singer, small-sized Clarence as Superman, and, of course, Starr in her exciting cowgirl costume — exciting until the evening proved too much so, because of our involvement in the Petros affair. A real stabbing, one that we thought affected us!

Then I remembered my bulky, and stunningly ugly, starched Red Cross uniform — and rejected the image immediately. I'm not as thin as I might be, and in that costume I appeared to be shaped something like a large Arizona barrel cactus.

At least the matter of Petros and the bloody knife had gradually been settled amicably, although not without a lot of effort. Would the problem of the Wet Bathing Suit ever reach that stage?

As I sat down in my trusty living room lift chair and pressed the lever to have my legs raised, I sighed with relief. Thank goodness for this comfort, I said to myself.

Now, what can I think of for Halloween that would be really different? If I got that matter settled, perhaps I could get back to work on my painting and my new mandala project. I permitted my mind to wander in the hope it would come up with an answer, thinking, too bad I don't have a mandala to use in order to reach this goal.

Instead of coming up with a solution for Halloween, I sank slowly into one of my visions of alternate reality. I saw myself standing on the rim of a volcano, as per the setting of the new Chris Markel movie I'd watched the previous evening. Peering into its fiery center, I realized that it promised to begin spitting lava at any moment. I tried to escape, but I couldn't move. And somehow I knew the man in the black cloak was coming to push me in. Chris escaped and left me there.

What could I do? I felt my arm grabbed and saw that the person who touched it was a shadowy woman in a black two-piece bathing suit. Who was she? It didn't matter; she was my way out. I was able to walk, with her support, down the steep outer side of the volcano, where we soon arrived at a beautiful blue-and-white tiled pool. She dived in and disappeared. I sat down at the edge, dangling my feet in the water. My legs felt good...

I came back to myself in my lift chair, where my legs did indeed feel good. Temporarily. But I seemed to be no closer to a solution of my costume problem. Thinking about my vision, I realized that the key to my extrication from the volcano was the bathing suit-clad woman. I wondered who she was.

The phone rang, and Katrina was reporting. "Mary Two had her hip operation while you were away and is coming home from rehab today," she announced. "A group of us are dining with her. Join us?"

I agreed gladly.

"Meet in the bar at six."

I decided I had better spend no more time today on the Halloween problem. I should work on my painting. I struggled out of the lift chair, massaging my stiff left knee and painful right wrist, and went into my studio, where I saw the protractor lying on a table. Pausing, I knew I really wanted to play with my new toy instead of working, so I did.

EIGHTEEN

The toy turned into a strict and demanding master, one that I obeyed gladly, having become completely absorbed in the project.

I worked for several days on my mandala, not replying to phone calls or email messages. I showed up very early for quick breakfasts, took only refrigerator snacks for lunch, and had my dinners delivered to my apartment. I even skipped my regular back exercises, though I regretted that later. I was holed up with my new project, and I didn't want to be distracted from it. I wanted to get it just right, because I planned to spend a lot of time using it.

I made one false start and discarded it. My next effort, prepared on 8 1/2 by 11 graph paper, embodied what I wanted. The center of my mandala contained three long petals. Around it sprouted tulip-like shapes with small spirals between them, and between the tulip shapes grew small square labyrinths. Another labyrinth provided a focus in the center of the image.

The result was something like a geometric design and something like a flower. It appealed to me, so I called my office supply store to order large sheets of Bristol board, in order to redo my mandala in a more impressive size and more permanent condition. When the office store could not fill my order, I phoned an artist's supply store, which delivered it the following day. Then I plunged into a creation of this mandala in a large format. I thought the result was striking. At that time, I didn't know quite how striking it looked.

Between my hours of work on the mandala, I took time to consider Halloween. At first I thought only of making myself into a large gold Buddha, but figuring out how to do that proved to be too daunting. Besides, who wants to admit to having a Buddha belly? Then I thought of something better... and easier. I started with a costume I bought and then fixed it up to my requirements. I got the main part of the job done in one evening. Then I returned to my new toy.

I would have been unable to create the rounded parts of my mandala accurately without the protractor, so I emailed Hugh that I was using his device daily—to good effect, I thought—and would return it when I was finished.

When I had finally completed the large-sized mandala to my satisfaction, I set aside an afternoon to try using it in meditation.

That morning I returned to my regular life. I replied to accumulated emails and answered phone messages. "Yes, I'm okay. I've been concentrating on work. I'll be in the bar this evening."

After a quick lunch of cheese and crackers, I set up my mandala on an easel standing in my living room opposite my trusty lift chair, where I sat down, got comfortable, and began centering my attention exclusively on the mandala.

I tried to be confident that this effort would work and I would reach my goal of becoming a meditator, a state which was supposed to contribute greatly to health. Deciding on my intention, I said it silently, and began immersing myself in the design I had created.

At first I had difficulty keeping out other thoughts: was that Halloween costume appropriate? Would the idea behind it disturb anyone? Did Ed survive his collapse? Is Helene doing any better in dealing with her depression? Is my current painting really any good? But gradually I was able to fix my attention solely on the mandala.

Pretty soon it began to whirl around—at least, it seemed to whirl. Then it began to get blurry. Again I was having a hard time keeping my thoughts where they belonged. Then my eyes began to close. I got too sleepy to look at the mandala, and I gave in, sat back, and napped.

Waking in time for dinner, I returned afterwards to watch a television movie on Turner Classics. After writing a short letter to a cousin in Cleveland, I retired at my usual time.

That was a terrible night. I'll never forget it. And it turned out so badly just because, having slept during the day, I woke up in the middle of the night and couldn't get back to sleep. This is a common enough phenomenon in people our age, but all too often it adds to our discomfort. By 2:00 A.M. I was hungry, so I picked up my flashlight, turned on a couple of living room lights, and went to the kitchen to start a piece of toast. When it popped up, I decided it wasn't dark enough, so I pushed it down again. Turning away to the fridge, I looked for something to spread on the toast.

That was when my smoke detector began to screech. Hastily, I turned off the toaster, watching wisps of smoke rise from it to the smoke detector on the ceiling directly above it. Grabbing a potholder, I took hold of the burned toast and threw it in the sink. With the potholder, I waved the smoke away from the detector.

The screeching stopped, but I knew I must have frightened a lot of people. I phoned Faisal, the night man at the front desk, identified myself and my apartment number, and began my explanation with "My toast burned and set off the smoke detector, but…"

Before I could say anything else he shouted, "I'll be right there!"

"No! It's all over. Nothing is burning!" But Faisal was obviously on his way. So I put on a robe and unlocked the door. There he was already! He must have run.

Under his arm he carried what looked like a Flit bug sprayer. As I began to explain that the danger was over, I saw that he was looking for a place to use his instrument. He already had his hand on the pusher, so I exclaimed, "Put that thing down! Did you think I have fleas?" I shouted.

"This is a water sprayer. Where is the fire?"

"There is no fire!"

"What's going on here? Is someone hurt?" Entering my apartment was Mrs. Cleghorn, a woman of about fifty, an experienced aide hired for night duty, whose job it was to take charge of any illness or injury after six in the evening. "Shall I phone for an ambulance?"

"No, no...."

"Oh my god, what's that?" Faisal had spotted my big mandala standing on the easel in the living room. Encountered in the half-light of two reading lamps, apparently to him it looked malevolent. "It's the devil's eye! And it's looking right at me! Let me out of here!"

His way out was blocked by Mrs. Cleghorn and also by Mr. Blackwood, who lived in the apartment across from mine and was standing barefoot on my prickly Welcome mat saying, "Ow! Ow!" and then "What's all this hubbub?" He was carrying his heavy blackthorn walking stick, which made me nervous to look at. Did he believe he would have to subdue someone?

He had dressed hurriedly, and one arm of his robe was inside out. It lay across his shoulder, showing more than I wanted to see of his orange-checked pajamas. He must have been sleeping on his starboard side, because all his hair was listing to port. This is an image I would have been glad to miss.

"Now Mr. Blackhead," began Mrs. Cleghorn.

"Black*wood*," he corrected, shaking his cudgel.

"Yes, let me help you back to your apartment, Mr. Blankhead."

"You are the one who needs help. Don't you know my name?"

"Arf! Arf! Arf!" Floozie walked in the door, sniffing unerringly in the direction of the counter where my toaster had done its best to make my life miserable. (I threw out that toaster the next day.) Floozie's owner must have opened her apartment door to see if she could figure out what all the noise was about, and Floozie walked out of it, following her nose.

"Please! Will everyone just leave? There is no need..." I begged.

Just then the phone rang. I picked up the receiver and set it down next to the base. That's one advantage to having an old-fashioned phone with the two functions separate, as I pointed out proudly the next day. You can indicate to the caller, by refusing to listen, that his call is unwelcome at that particular moment.

By then Faisal had managed to push his way out. He never entered my apartment again, convinced that I was harboring something demonic.

Mrs. Cleghorn gradually persuaded Mr. Blankhead, or Blankwood, to leave, which he did while making a few more "Ow" sounds while walking across my Welcome mat. For a moment I considered discarding that mat because the message it sent to passers-by was less true than it had been earlier.

During all this time, while I kept asking them all to leave, I must have sounded piteous, for eventually Mrs. Cleghorn patted me on the shoulder and murmured, "Now, don't you worry, dear, everything's all right," but her remark merely made me angry, because it stated something I already knew and had been trying to tell them for some time.

Finally, Floozie was the only one left with Mrs. Cleghorn and me. She sat down, seemingly waiting for something, probably food. At the door, Mrs. Cleghorn turned and noticed her. "Now, Floozie, where is it you live? I will have to get you back there."

"Arf," said Floozie, but that didn't help.

"I guess I'll have to look up your owner's apartment number." Mrs. Cleghorn turned to me. "Do you have your Residents' List handy, dear?"

"No," I lied. "I have no idea where it is."

"Well, then. Come on, Floozie. We'll have to go to the office." And she picked up the dog. "Good night, dear."

I was so upset that I didn't even answer.

On my way to bed I heard an insistent electronic beeping and recalled that I had neglected to replace the phone receiver. For a moment I considered throwing that thing out, too, but I thought better of it.

The next morning I devised a cleaned-up version of this story in order to tell it at breakfast. The story wasn't nearly as colorful as reality, but it showed clearly that, far from being the wrong-doer, I was the victim.

NINETEEN

While I was recovering from my traumatic Night of the Burned Toast, I knew I had to start thinking of preparing to exhibit at the Locksley Glen Art Show. But something nice happened to intervene. I got a date.

Well, not exactly a date. A lot of others were invited.

Hugh called to invite me to a cocktail party at his apartment. "I planned it to coincide with the Art Show," he explained, "because I'm inviting people to view the two new Goswell paintings I bought. Since I can't create art, at least I can participate by showing I appreciate other people's art."

I knew Hugh was long-winded, from the first time I met him, and he was demonstrating it once again.

"Besides, I could tell you were reluctant to visit me at my apartment alone. The apartment will be jammed with people that evening. Please come."

He must have sensed that I harbored an old-fashioned embarrassment about going alone to a man's apartment. That's a legacy of having been brought up in the 1930s. It must be rule number 75 that said, "Never go to a man's apartment if you will be alone with him."

It was clever of Hugh to use the art show as an occasion for displaying the art he had just bought. I was glad to accept.

"I'm calling it a reception so that people won't feel they have to stay long. I expect guests to leave whenever they like. Come right after the show, when it closes at 4:30."

"I look forward to it." And I really did.

Then another stimulating event occurred: I received an email message from the two young sociologists I'd met in San Francisco. They were following through with their idea of studying housing options for the elderly, and they asked if they could interview me about the way I solved it for myself.

I felt quite set up by this evidence that my knowledge might be valued by experts in the field. I replied that I was willing to be interviewed, if they could devise a list of questions I might answer not on the phone but through email.

I gave my reason: in my experience of being interviewed about my painting, I had long ago learned that off-the-cuff answers to serious questions, which are needed for phone interviews, never seemed satisfactory later because they lacked the depth that time to think might have given them. The sociologists agreed to send me their questions within a few days. Meanwhile, I took the opportunity of learning about the sociologists themselves.

First, I had to learn how to address them. All I knew, from a printed list that Dr. Kano had given out, is that they were Dr. Wang and Dr. Yao, instructors in sociology at the University of Vancouver in British Columbia, Canada. But which was the woman and which the man? I'm ashamed to admit that although I had dinner with them every evening for five nights, I never bothered to get that straight; I just addressed both of them as "Doctor."

So I looked them up on the internet and learned that the woman was Dr. Nicole "Nikki" Wang, and her husband was Dr. Stephen Yao. It was a relief to learn that they had Western given names, so I wouldn't have to memorize two more Chinese names.

It was also good to notice that in corresponding with them I wouldn't have to write "Wang Nikki" or "Yao Stephen," in the Chinese style of address — family name first, because I had often wondered: when you type the name in Chinese fashion, where do you put the title? I'll never have to learn that.

Hurrah! One thing fewer to learn. And how refreshing that, although married, the woman kept her own last name. Many Americans are only now getting used to that practice.

The two vowel letters at the end of "Yao" worried me a bit. If I ever spoke on the phone to Dr. Yao, I would need to pronounce his name right. There was no Chinese consulate in Naples where I could inquire about correct pronunciation, so I fell back on the internet again and discovered a site explaining how to pronounce the name. It even included a short recording illustrating the pronunciation as "Yah-oh."

Good. I practiced it.

How handy the internet can be, even for people my age. I felt quite up-to-date with my solution.

I was ready to face the sociologists' questions, I thought. Then I received them. Whoa! Their depth and significance intimidated me. I knew a lot of answers, I realized, but they were not always positive ones. I wondered if my replies would startle them or turn them away from the project.

I might tell them things they may not want to know, things that indicate how stressful the decisions affecting our final years can be. I decided, however, that I'd have to be honest, whether or not my replies fit the view of aging that these people had in their minds.

When they asked me, for example, whether my adult children helped me locate the institution where I live, I had to explain that I had no children, adult or otherwise, thus showing them that they had made an unwarranted assumption. I hoped they weren't insulted by my correcting them.

I also pointed out that adult children's participation in this decision, however well meant, could be questionable. I knew that the children of some other residents had taken part in their selection of a place to live, but whether to call their participation "help" or not had to be considered a matter of opinion. I wrote that I could tell a lot of stories about this matter, and I told one.

It's common for adult children to believe that their parents cannot make their own decisions about where to live, so the children choose a place for them. This happened to a woman I'll call Josephine, whose children made the trip to Naples without her and picked out the facility, and even the apartment, they liked for their mother.

If Mom had been affected by memory problems, that might have been excusable, but she wasn't. She was confined to a wheelchair because of severe neuropathy in her legs.

Josephine's children selected for their mom an apartment in a quiet corner of the building, with windows overlooking a lovely pond where wildlife could often be observed. The children assumed that quiet surroundings were appropriate for her in her declining years. But within a week Josephine, who came from New York City, said she was ready to move out. She was used to action. Nothing happened within view of her new apartment.

When the rental agent heard she wanted to leave and why, he realized that he had the right place for her: an apartment directly over the main entrance, where all day long, cars and vans drove up and released passengers or took them in, where delivery companies brought in the mail and packages, and where the chatting and shouting of visiting children could often be heard. It was a lively scene. He moved Josephine to her new apartment, where she was very happy.

Some adult children "permit" their parents to participate in making the decision. This attitude is demeaning. It's part of the view of old people as weak in the head and lacking in ability to live in the world. Many younger people see us this way. In their minds, we are essentially children, who need direction, advice, and supervision.

Some retirees, when they observe that their children have placed them in this stereotype, assume the children are right and let themselves sink right into it.

That's not what we need. What we need is love. Translate that as concern and offers to help with anything, and the children will be on the right track.

That's what I was writing when three taps on the door announced Hilda, my aide, who then used her key to enter my apartment, calling out cheerily, "It's seven A.M. on Wednesday, Mrs. D, time for your weekly shower!" So that was all for the questionnaire until after breakfast.

TWENTY

Katrina seemed to have given up on the idea that Aidan was a violent person. "I doubt it strongly."

"You're influenced by Helene," Annabelle said. "She's critical of everyone, yet she can't seem to grasp that some people are evil. Doesn't she read the newspaper?"

I changed the subject. "How about an update on Ed Champion?"

Katrina responded. "He's home. He was just dehydrated. On the other hand, Clarence is still in the hospital. Complications of having his pacemaker adjusted."

"Joan's with him?"

"Yes. Clarence wanted to submit some sketches to the Art Show. Joan gave me a key to their apartment so I could see that Jimmy's men collect them at 1:30 for display in the Big Game Room."

"Mine are being picked up at one. I'm leaving here after the soup."

"Are they the mandalas you've been telling us about?"

I nodded.

"I wish I had paid more attention to your explanations," Annabelle admitted. "I can't recall much about them."

"See if you like them before you ask for another explanation," I warned. "They're different from anything I've ever done."

Back at my apartment, while waiting for Jimmy's men I took the opportunity of considering the next question from the sociologists: "How about financing this kind of life? Isn't assisted living expensive?"

Yes, too expensive for my husband and me (I wrote). I wouldn't be living here today if my husband hadn't several years ago proposed that we buy long-term care insurance. We were lucky that an insurance agent lived in the cottage adjacent to the one we owned in Naples, because that's where we learned about long-term care insurance. That insurance ultimately made it possible for us to live in Locksley Glen.

We paid into the insurance for five years before we realized that we needed some daily help in our home, so we applied for it, submitting the required statement from our doctors, so our insurance covered the cost of the help. In fact, with the assistance of the insurance we stayed in our cottage for ten years before deciding we had to leave in favor of full-time care. Running the house and handling the fruit trees had gotten to be too much, even with part-time help, because we both had so many limitations. We looked for assisted living and found Locksley Glen, which is one of several such places in Naples.

It's a good idea (I explained to the sociologists) to visit more than one of these facilities in order to compare them on the basis of a list of your requirements for happiness. People who have a solid, realistic list can make judgments on the basis of their specific needs.

I was on the verge of typing an example of such a list for Doctors Wang and Yao when two of Jimmy's men arrived with a mover's cart to transport my mandalas, all wrapped and ready, along with the little signs I had prepared. One of Jimmy's men was Jimmy himself, and the other was a wiry woman called Flo, who was certainly as strong as Jimmy.

The two of them did their thing, and I locked my apartment, trailing along behind as they left so that I could see my compositions safely mounted in the Big Game Room.

That evening I opened Annabelle's folder with trepidation. Would her writing style appear to be too poor to improve? Would she use some of her odd expressions, like the one in which she claimed her life was an open bush? Would I have to tell her I thought she had no chance of publication?

I hate doing that.

Luckily, that wasn't the case. I merely pointed out the usual problems of misplaced modifiers, missing antecedents, and use of an inappropriate word. Occasionally, I smiled to myself when I could mark a few sentences with the "bird noise," AWK, when they sounded awkward and needed revision for clarity. The organization of her material worked well except for the last section, which appeared to meander, so I made some suggestions for altering it. As for her design ideas, I found them original and refreshing.

Well, I thought, good for Annabelle. And I'll bet she's feeling happier, too. I wrote a congratulatory note and slipped it into her folder. Then I walked over to the group of pigeonholes used for internal correspondence and inserted the folder in the one labeled with her apartment number.

At breakfast I saw Annabelle across the room. She waved me over with a big smile.

Katrina spoke first. "Annabelle likes your editing."

"You're a real writer, Annabelle. I was surprised at your skill. If you fix up those problems I've marked, you'll have something ready to submit."

"I really appreciate your work, Alice One. Thanks for all this help."

"It's what friends are for."

What is it about doing things for people that is so gratifying? I guess it makes us feel good because we are contributing something to the world.

TWENTY-ONE

If Starr hadn't come to the Annual Locksley Glen Art Show, we might never have solved the mystery of the Wet Bathing Suit.

I was standing near my third mandala when she came in looking elegant in a black taffeta cocktail gown with a wide neckline, where she displayed a lot of skin decorated with onyx jewelry. She looked at the compositions with surprise.

"These are the ones? My goodness, they are unusual! I can't believe they're yours. Usually, what you paint is representational. You explained that to me once."

"I think a Martian painted them," declared Lucas. "They're nothing like your usual style. How in the world did you come up with this idea?"

I tried to explain, but others were arriving to look and comment. I moved away a bit, and I heard Annabelle say, "They can't be hers. Look again at the name."

"They're hers, all right," said Ed. "Unless she's signed her name to somebody else's work."

"Don't be silly, Ed," Katrina said. "Don't you recall her description of mandalas? These are the ones."

Then Starr remarked quietly to me, "I've seen something like this before."

"Yes," I said, "in the Asian Art Museum."

"No, I mean more recently."

"Recently? Where have you been recently?"

Not replying directly, she murmured, "Something with a black background. And the mandala was small."

"A small mandala with a black background?" I countered. "I can't imagine where it was."

"I'll think of it," she said, and turned toward my compositions again. "I like them. They're dramatic."

"So do I," Katrina said. "So unusual. They're stunning. I'll have to learn more about them and how they are made. They must be difficult to create."

Then Adrian came up behind Katrina. I moved away a bit, ostensibly to give him room to view my work but really because I still felt a bit frightened of him. He looked but said nothing, then walked over to see Clarence's sketches, where he spent no more than a minute and moved on.

Clarence had made two sketches of the boys, Petros and Stavros—or Steve, as he preferred to be known—whom he was supervising for the county's Department of Social Services. Examining the sketches, I recalled that the boys were twins, although not identical. In one picture the boys were looking at each other curiously. In the other—the one I preferred—Petros was looking at the artist with a happy smile, and Stavros stood with a three-quarters turn toward the artist. His eyes were narrowed and his mouth showed a soft smile of pleasure.

"What charming pictures! It's how I remember the two boys. Will they be here to see this?"

Joan, standing guard at Clarence's art work, replied, "Tomorrow afternoon. They can both be here then. And so will Clarence. He's coming home tonight." I told her how glad I was and how delightful the sketches were.

Then I toured the room. Hermione Kreutzer had a table with five necklaces to show, all carefully designed and constructed. I knew she had a good chance to win the annual art prize, as she had done the previous year. She sat at the table proudly, wearing a sixth necklace made of stunning cabochons set in silver. Residents clustered at her exhibit.

At a round table were the three judges — two women and a man — all from the Naples Art Museum, talking with each other about the submissions, probably trying to influence each other. How else would they all agree on the best art? I had to admit that everything was of high quality, including some abstract paintings with large splashes of color, painted by Mr. Blockwood. Bluntwood? Flatwood? Why can't I remember his name? Probably some mental block against names made of compound words.

I'd never cared for abstract work, but I had to admit that Mr. Blandwood's compositions were carefully done and interesting. For drapes or upholstery. Maybe carpeting.

Hugh didn't arrive until afternoon. Instead of the ubiquitous tan sports jacket he appeared in a pale gray tropical suit and looked quite handsome, although he limped a bit. His eyebrows looked bushier than ever. His friend Paul Benes accompanied him. As for me, I wore my usual black velvet and pearls, and Hugh complimented me on my appearance, then went off with Paul to view the art.

That's when Starr came up to me. It was about three o'clock. This was an important moment, and I still recall how startled I was when she said, "I've remembered where I saw a mandala recently, a small one. On a black background."

"Where?"

"On the two-piece black bathing suit."

For a moment I was silent. "No. Really?"

"Yes. Remember when we went to examine the Lost and Found box? Clarence was grabbing at everything in it. He was very nervous. When he finally found the suit, he couldn't seem to examine it. Too shaky. I told him to step aside, that I would do it."

"Yes?"

"As I was looking for the seam with the label that gave the name of the manufacturer and the size, my fingers felt something else. Something round and hard. I thought it was a button. It was pinned or sewn to the neckline of the bra section. A small mandala. A decoration."

"Oh. A small mandala. And you just remembered seeing that?"

"Yes. It wasn't until now that I recognized it as a mandala. If we hadn't been to the Asian Art Museum, I probably wouldn't have. I paid little attention to the button, or pin, on the bathing suit because Clarence's condition made me want to get him back to his apartment quickly. I was afraid he might have a fit right in front of us."

I took a breath. I hadn't heard that expression in a long time. When I was a child, everyone feared "having a fit," but nobody knew exactly what that meant because we'd never seen it happen.

There I go, thinking of my childhood again.

I said to Starr, "What do you think this means?"

"I think the person who owns that mandala button or pin has more of them and uses them as decorations on her other clothes."

I was stupefied. I stood there saying nothing.

I remembered feeling like that once before, when at the last Halloween Party I saw blood on Starr's knife, and I waddled forward in my starched Red Cross uniform to see if she was hurt, although I knew full well that the knife I had helped her make was constructed from cardboard.

So even though I might not act stupefied, I know what stupefied feels like.

Finally, I was able to respond to Starr's insight.

"How did you come up with this idea?"

"I don't know. It just seems true."

"You mean, all we have to do is find a woman who owns buttons or pins that represent mandalas?"

"It seems so."

"Do you want to start looking for her?"

"I'm already looking. I've been touring the room and looking at women's chests." She giggled. "Clarence's son is a policeman, so maybe I'll be arrested soon. If I am, will you bail me out?"

I couldn't help laughing. "Next thing you know, I'll catch you searching for vibrator museums."

We both stood there laughing. People started to turn their heads toward us. We finally realized that onlookers might believe we were laughing at someone's art, so we moved into the hallway in order to recover our aplomb, if we ever had any. If it's worth recovering. That's just a metaphor, of course. I'm not sure what aplomb looks like.

While we were talking, Hugh came along, and we realized it was time for his reception. He reminded us before he left that we would be expected soon. I headed for my apartment in order to freshen up, and Starr went back into the Big Game Room to search further, she said, for Big Game.

In about twenty minutes I was standing in front of one of the Ridley Goswell paintings in Hugh's apartment when Starr waltzed into the open door. I realized that instead of wearing the banned flip-flops, she had put on some patent pumps with three-inch heels, which were about as popular with the head nurse as flip-flops.

The nurse was also the facility's Safety Officer, so she was on the lookout for things like inappropriate shoes, which contributed considerably to the incidence of falling.

As Starr walked toward me in those ridiculous shoes, something clicked in my head. I realized that I knew what my painting was missing: footprints. To decide their placement, I needed to view the scene once more. For some reason, viewing that scene seemed urgent, so I told Hugh I'd return, went back to my apartment for my sketch pad and charcoal pencil, stuffed them in my purse, and departed for the pool patio.

There I stood staring at a brick path that led away from a chaise longue. In my mind I could picture footprints on the path, so I sketched it from one end to the other. I even added outlines of footprints where I believed they should be.

Finally, it was all coming together. I wanted to get back to my painting to work on this last section, but I had to return to Hugh's party.

TWENTY-TWO

At Hugh's reception I felt unaccountably drawn to the Ridley Goswell painting with the line of treelike objects along the left side. I had begun to find it appealing, and I had to admit this to Hugh as soon as I had the opportunity. "I thought you weren't coming back," he responded. "I'm so glad you did. There's someone I want you to meet." He led me to the other side of the living room, squeezing through bodies packed tightly. Nobody seemed to want to leave. "Matthew, excuse me. Alice, I want you to meet my son Matthew. Matt, Mrs. Dennison. And this is my daughter-in-law, Ah Lam."

"You are the artist?" Matthew asked. "How wonderful."

"I love your work with mandalas, Mrs. Dennison," said his wife. How did you become so proficient in making them? And where did you learn that skill?" I was charmed by Ah Lam's interest, her respectfulness in avoiding use of my first name, and her sleek appearance in a peach-colored cheongsam, as well as by Matthew's resemblance to his father. In a few moments we were deep in conversation.

Soon the noise of people talking grew very loud and intrusive. Hugh interrupted Ah Lam to ask me to stay after the reception and have dinner with him and his family. But I was getting tired; it had been a long day. I knew I'd have to get off my feet soon, and I dearly wanted to lie down. So I asked if another time would be possible. Hugh said yes, we would do it tomorrow instead. I made my goodbyes and thankyous.

That evening, after talking to Starr on the phone and while soaking my tired feet, I made several calls to residents about Starr's discovery of a button or pin on the Wet Bathing Suit and her subsequent insight. Starr herself spoke to both Clarence and Joan. Pretty soon we had gotten the attention of the whole group, and we agreed to think of ways to follow up on Starr's discovery. We decided to convene at lunch to discuss… our stralogy.

In the morning Patricia Knightsbridge called at nine to tell me she was coming to see the mandalas. "I hardly know what they are, though I think I saw some in New York's Metropolitan Museum of Art long ago. I'll read up on them before coming, so I'll know what I'm looking at."

I tried to get some work done on my still life, but I was distracted by Starr's persuasive theory and spent most of the morning trying to think of ways to discreetly find out who had a collection of mandala buttons or pins. Number of ways I thought of? Zero.

At noon a group of us gathered for lunch. "We can't just go around asking every woman we know, can we?" Annabelle worried.

"How can you be so sure, Starr, that there are other such buttons or pins?" asked Ed.

"Because buttons are always sold in multiples of about six. Even if these are really not buttons but pins that are sold one at a time, the makers are likely to offer other versions of the same product, since manufacturers know that customers want choices of different designs."

"Where could such buttons or pins be bought?"

"In museum shops," I replied. "I visit them at every opportunity. These shops offer copies of the originals seen in the museums. They're very popular, so they've become lucrative sources of income for institutions."

"Back to stralogy," said Annabelle. She appeared to be using that word both for "strategy" and for "astrology," so we followed suit. "Maybe for a while we should just watch what women are using for decorations on their jackets and dresses. Later, if that doesn't seem to work, we can consider asking right out who has a collection of mandala pins or buttons."

"Smart. Let's be restrained at first. Maybe we'll get the answer without asking."

This was the second and final day of the art exhibit. I waited until afternoon to attend. It was at the end of this day that we would learn who had won the prize for the best art.

At about 2:00, along came Clarence with the two young men. It was clear that they weren't boys any more. After all, Petros worked as a waiter, and Stavros was a college student. They appeared to be fine, upstanding young fellows. Clarence must be doing a good job mentoring them, I thought.

Katrina and I were standing at the entrance, so we gave them welcoming smiles, shook their hands, and escorted them immediately to Clarence's sketches, leaving them with Joan while we toured the room for the umpteenth time.

Starr and Annabelle, too, were walking around and around looking at women's blouses and watching their faces for signs of recognition as they viewed the three mandalas. Mary Two, in pain from her recent operation, left at 2:30.

Patricia Knightsbridge made her entrance in a white suit and pumps, stopped to say hello, and then marched straight to the mandalas. "Well, I'll be scuppered," she exclaimed, and I remembered she came from a fishing family in Maine. "What a switcheroo! You do know this is geometric art, don't you, Alice?"

"I guess," I admitted reluctantly. "I can't really say why it appeals to me, except perhaps to use as a method of meditation."

"Which you are now doing?"

"Nope. Not yet. Maybe soon."

"I'm just amazed. And pleased, of course. How about letting me take them? I'd love to represent you with these, Alice, at the usual terms, and I'd be proud to have them in my gallery."

"Eventually, Patricia. Give me time to try using them as they were meant to be used."

"Okay. But not forever. I'll be pestering you by phone. And I'm still curious about the painting you've supposedly been working on for about a year. When, when, when will it be ready?"

"Soon. I think I finished it late last night, but I need a few days to know for sure."

"So it really exists. Okay. Keep in touch."

When Bob Avery came in, some of us watched him, not because of the mandalas but because he had so often admitted his appreciation for women in scanty bathing suits. We could tell, however, that his interest did not extend to mandalas, for he looked at them in surprise, backed up, looked them up and down again, and walked away.

Maybe he agrees with Faisal.

Then Shelley came in. She wore a green dress, and around her throat was a necklace of brown wooden beads. No pin. She walked over to the mandalas. I thought her reaction to them was peculiar. She smiled, then frowned, and finally walked away. "Was that a smile of recognition?" I asked Katrina.

"It seemed like one to me. But why frown?"

"Can't imagine."

Several of us strolled around checking out all the women who came in, but none of us saw anything worth reporting.

Then it was four o'clock, and the judges were preparing to announce the winner. One of the men tapped a gavel and asked for quiet. After a short speech praising the submissions, he declared that the winner of the Locksley Glen Art Prize was Alice Dennison, for her works, "Three Mandalas." All my friends clapped, and Ed cheered.

The judge presented me with a trophy about a foot high and not very well designed, but I thanked the Naples Art Museum graciously, I hope. I admit that sometimes I'm unnecessarily critical, but if I'm going to display the trophy in my studio... Never mind.

Brett Bozeman gave me a hug of congratulations, and so did Starr. Hugh shook my hand. I saw his son and daughter-in-law in the audience, clapping. It was a very nice moment.

Now, I thought, I must learn how to use these mandalas. But first I had to oversee the transport of my three compositions to my apartment, then get ready for my pickup by Hugh and his family at 5:30.

Good things were happening. And maybe we were closer to identifying the owner of the Wet Bathing Suit. Stralogy.

That evening Hugh's son Matthew drove us to the Marco Polo Restaurant, where we enjoyed Italian food and more good talk. I learned that Ah Lam had heard of "Wang and Yao," as she referred to them, because of their scholarly articles, although Ah Lam was not a sociologist but a historian. I also discovered that I was mentally pronouncing "Wang" incorrectly — so I had been concentrating on getting the wrong family name right — because Ah Lam pronounced it with the "ah" vowel, as if it was spelled Wong. Mentally, I corrected myself.

I also learned that Matthew had once worked for his father (Hugh, it appeared, was an engineer) but now ran his own business. Hugh kept steering the conversation back to art, and we talked a lot about the multiple collections in "the Met," the New York Metropolitan Museum of Art.

When Katrina asked me later about my "date" with Hugh, I responded that I believed I'd been asked to join his family outing not for myself but because Hugh loves art and enjoys contacts with people he calls "real artists."

But that's better than not being asked at all.

TWENTY-THREE

The weather had for a month been dreadful, with heavy tropical storms every day, some of them electrical. Once in a while a lightning strike would disable all our lights, computers, and televisions for a few hours while the cable company sent out its workers to set things aright.

We thought little of this. After all, it was the Naples hurricane season. Those of us who had been residents for at least a year were used to the tropical autumn. We stayed inside most of the time, engaging in activities that didn't require going outside.

When in early October the weather channel began showing us images of large storms approaching Southwest Florida, we kept track of them daily, but each time, they moved off to the north before approaching hurricane force. Occasionally, we experienced storms with strong winds, but nothing our building couldn't handle.

Our minds as well as our bodies turned inward. We prepared for, and enjoyed, activities like the art show. Beach picnics got cancelled, and so did motor trips to nearby tourist sites. Few people felt like shopping, and the Glen van traveled nearly empty to Trader Joe's. So we checked on each other's health, rounded up friends to join us in parties, and shared juicy novels as well as CDs that furnished thrilling music. More people showed up for the nightly movies. Even Bingo had a spurt of popularity, and with the increased number of players, the winner's pot got larger.

We heard talk of creative costumes being prepared for the Halloween Party, so we began to anticipate fun that evening.

Ed Champion was taking care of his hydration, causing an increase in the consumption of mint juleps. His use of a Kentucky accent appeared or disappeared depending on the occasion. Helene was hanging on at Locksley Glen, maybe because she realized that we wanted to keep her around to talk to and because Lucas kept encouraging her. We often called to request her royal presence at dinner, and sometimes she even came.

Mary Two was recuperating from her operation, but slowly. Older people like us take extra time to heal. Clarence had recovered from an anomaly concerning his heart: that was all we knew about it. Annabelle was sticking to her plan to practice her guitar daily and waiting to learn whether her design ideas would find a publisher.

Aidan hadn't moved out yet but seemed restless, walking the halls to keep his muscles toned. Few people invited him to join them at dinner. Only Shelley seemed still devoted to him. When we saw them in the Dining Room together, we altered our approach in order to pass their table and check out what Shelley was wearing. "If she owns mandala pins, she's keeping them in their box," Annabelle said. "I'm beginning to think I'll have to ask her right out whether she has them. After all, I'm the only one who has actually dined with her." She meant the only one of our group. Shelley was making other friends, too.

Astrid avoided Aidan, and soon her husband reappeared at their two-person dining table. Bob's wounds healed, and he became less self-conscious about his experience of falling in the bathroom. Starr said she was performing research on purse and luggage design, in preparation for some kind of assignment from the Denver designer. Katrina was everywhere, supporting everyone, despite the hated Boot.

As for my still life, I was putting the finishing touches on it when the Big Storm came on the horizon.

We watched the sea charts shown on TV as Hurricane Gaylord approached the Caribbean, where it struck on a Sunday and slowed its movement as it encountered land, knocking down trees and power lines on several islands. Amazingly, nobody was hurt.

Then Hurricane Gaylord backed down. Its winds lessened their speed, and it seemed to be petering out.

After a day it picked up speed and aimed straight for us. When that happened, we received a message from Director Grambling: he was calling us all to a meeting in the Big Game Room at 1:00, right after lunch, to talk about the coming storm.

Not that we were really worried. Locksley Glen was safe through a Force Three hurricane. Residents had never needed to leave the building for a safer one. Naples contained no safer building, anyway, so if ours proved untenable, we would have to be bussed out of town.

I thought only of protecting my paintings; nothing else was of great value to me. And they were safer in my apartment than at Patricia's gallery, which was closer to the ocean and faced East, where storms usually entered Southwest Florida. I was keeping my paintings in my care.

At 12:50 the Big Game Room was crowded. Walkers and electric scooters lined two walls as residents struggled to sit down, trying to suppress the groans that erupted when stress was put on knees and hips.

Director Grambling stilled the murmurings in the room when he entered and said, "Good afternoon. I called you in so you could be assured that we are completely prepared if Hurricane Gaylord comes anywhere near Naples."

Chef Alejandro stirred in his chair. He felt his tall chef's hat drooping a little to one side, so he righted it. Chef knew that much of the preparedness Director Grambling mentioned would depend on him. No matter the weather outside, Locksley Glen residents would want to eat, and they wouldn't be satisfied with bread and water.

The director continued: "We are ready for anything. We have a list of employees who are willing to stay overnight in the building, for a period of days if necessary, in order to take care of you, handling the entire range of resident requirements. All senior staff will be here every night. Our stock of food supplies contains all the prepared food, canned food, and dried food that the state government requires, plus much more, and all the required water."

Chef sat up straighter, and a confident look spread over his face. He looked around him, smiling and nodding agreement. Like everyone, he enjoyed recognition.

"Remember that we have backup power to operate lights and air conditioning, and the ambulance is located just down the street, ready to respond to emergencies. So there is nothing to worry about. Just go about your regular activities. Just keep any required meds handy. If the storm becomes acute, we may ask you to move yourself into the hallways, the ones with no windows to break. Chairs and cots will be furnished. Any questions?"

Of course, there were several, all of them already covered in Director Grambling's talk, which some residents could not take in all at once. So he repeated many of his assurances, and most residents left the meeting satisfied, although they tried to find something to mutter about when they reached the hallway. The last objection I heard, from Mr. Blackthorn, or Blackbird, was "And how would we get to the bathroom?" which was answered facetiously by Jimmy DiParisi: "They'll bring you a potty."

It was raining hard, so I figured this to be the perfect time to try meditating with one of my mandalas, and I made full preparations to do so. I set up one of my compositions on an easel right in front of my lift chair, then settled into my seat and tried to relax.

Usually, I used music, especially Mozart or Beethoven, to relax and lower my blood pressure. But meditation is supposed to have multiple health benefits beyond lowering that important number, and I wanted—well, maybe not desperately, but strongly—to teach myself to do it.

I took several deep breaths, thought briefly of a goal I wanted to reach, then began clearing my mind of all thoughts. To help me do that, I imagined a clear white space, like a canvas with nothing on it. For a while my mind cleared. Then I began focusing on my mandala. My eyes traveled here and there in the design, finally settling on the center. I took more deep breaths, thinking: the center, the center, the center holds my intention.

The mandala began whirling, or seemed to, and then I sank into one of my visions of alternate reality. It was not unlike others I've experienced. I was at the pool again, and this time the wind came up. The tops of nearby palm trees waved. Thunder rumbled. Aidan was in the pool. Annabelle, wearing the black bathing suit, came to tell Aidan to get out of the pool, unless he wanted to be hit by lightning. Aidan replied, "You aren't the one," and turned his back. Then the vision faded.

I felt tired. The vision not only seemed unhelpful and illogical, it failed to relate to my intention. It's just like my same old imaginings of alternate reality. Fooey, I thought, selecting a word from my childhood, one that had come in handy when my Popsicle dropped on the sidewalk.

Then I reconsidered: I'm probably doing it all wrong. I'll have to order some more books on the subject. Perhaps the one I found is incomplete. If other people can do it, so can I. Meanwhile, I'll go finish my Halloween costume instead.

That was a better idea. I heard thunder starting again, so I knew I couldn't take a walk around the campus or go to the pool court to relax. Moving my mind to Halloween was just the ticket. I shut down my laptop computer so that it would not attract lightning and pulled out the costume I had been working on.

Suddenly, I thought of another addition that should be made to my still life. I put the costume away and went back to my painting, trying to figure out the best place to make my addition. When I located the right spot, I mixed my colors and got to work. I wasn't distracted by the lightning that lit up the sky.

TWENTY-FOUR

It was party day, and my costume was ready. The weather was rotten, but we weren't going anywhere. The storm named Graybeard, or GoDaddy, or something like that, had drawn off to one side and was petering out, leaving our whole area awash in large puddles.

Hannah the Hairdresser had seen to it that my hair was precisely the shade of beige that I like. Moreover, I came away from the beauty salon that morning with a new insight: the realization that Hannah had become one of the most important people at Locksley Glen. She took it as part of her job to jolly grouchy women into improving their tempers, managing this by teasing them about their attitude until they actually laughed.

The beauty salon was one of the most popular destinations in the building. People without appointments popped in all day long, with excuses like asking for a piece of candy, needing a tissue, inquiring whether Hannah had a postage stamp or a needle and thread, pleading to borrow cash from her, and asking when their next appointment was. Once I heard a resident begging for a back rub.

Some forgot that they had been beautified the day before and showed up again to be worked on. Others came to read glamour magazines, taking up space in dryer chairs needed by wet-headed residents horned with blue curlers.

Hannah's helpfulness was legendary. Women arrived, often with their daughters or sons, to thank her for working on her days off in order to glamorize them for celebrations like Mother's Day or Christmas or to prepare them for visits from relatives.

If a woman lost her earrings, eyeglasses, purse, or house key, it was Hannah who seemed to know where in her apartment she should look for it. When a resident forgot to show up for her appointment, Hannah might appear on her doorstep and, if necessary, help her out of bed and into some clothing.

Men who were nearly hairless came to see Hannah ostensibly for haircuts but actually just to talk to Hannah, who was always upbeat. So-called support people like Hannah, I realized, were essential cogs in the wheels of progress at Locksley Glen, although I wasn't sure what a cog looked like or why a wheel needed one.

Getting ready to leave Hannah's shop, I was packing into a canvas carryall the papers and magazines I had brought along to read when I spied a green enameled box on the counter next to the Priceless Polished Princess Hair Conditioner and the Sunny Blonde English Colourant. "What a pretty box, Hannah. Is it new?"

"I just bought it yesterday. I decided I needed a place to store all the earrings and hearing aids people take off and leave here. You can peek inside." She was doing a comb-out on Minnie of the Golden Cane, so I opened the box myself. Inside lay one large and circular silver bangle, a pair of turquoise danglers, a round black-and-white pin, and...

A round black-and-white pin? I decided to examine it more closely and picked it up.

"Found something of yours?" asked Hannah.

"No, just something I admire." And I kept examining it until I was certain: yes, it was a small black mandala about an inch and a half across, about a half-inch thick. On the back had been glued a fastener that resembled a safety pin. The delicate design on the front had been painted on with a very fine brush.

I replaced the pin in the green box. "Whose pin is that?" I asked.

"Don't know. Found it on the floor one day last week. You have no idea whose it is?"

"Nope. But I wish I did."

"If anyone claims it, I'll let you know. Bye, Love." And I was dismissed.

I walked quickly, or at least relatively quickly, to my apartment, where I phoned Starr and reported my find. "You were right," I admitted.

"Of course I was right," she announced. "Am I ever wrong?"

I laughed. "Only when insisting that we should visit a vibrator museum."

"Oh, you have enough vibrators already, do you?" she teased.

"That's enough of that. Got your costume ready?"

"Yes, but I'm not inviting you here to see it. Last year, your visit didn't result in a good Halloween party."

She referred to the cowgirl costume she had laid out on her white sofa on the occasion of my visit, a costume that Petros had spotted while passing by, and one that inspired him to hide a bloody knife there.

"Okay, Podner. So long," I said, echoing a phrase I remembered from last year's party.

I turned to my own costume, but before I put it on I thought of something else. Phoning Hairdresser Hannah, I asked permission to borrow something from her green box: a round black pin decorated in white.

"Why not? Nobody seems to have missed it. C'mon over."

So I did. Annabelle was getting her fluffy hair fluffed, and she was curious as to my reason for being there. I picked up the green box and looked in. The pin was still there, so I put it in my purse. "Just borrowing this for my Halloween costume," I told Annabelle. "Stop looking."

"Okay, okay. I want to be surprised, anyway."

I spotted a paperback novel in Annabelle's hands, so I asked what she was reading. "*Of Human Bondage* by Somerset Mayhem," she replied. "It's not very good. Just a bunch of third-rate painters… Oops!"

"Oops is right" was my parting shot. "Not enough mayhem, of course."

On the way back home I heard a piano being played in Bill Hufferman's apartment, and I recalled that he had not entertained us during Happy Hour for a while. I wondered why. I would soon learn.

It was time to suit up. Instead of getting out of my normal clothes, I left them on and donned my costume on top of them, pulling it over my head. I had bought one of those large plastic bags with a hole at the closed end for the head and two armholes at the sides.

On it someone had painted (rather ineptly) a front view of the body of a buxom young woman wearing a two-piece black bathing suit. On the back of the bag was painted the back view of the same half-dressed young body in the same bathing suit.

When I approach someone while wearing this costume, the supposed effect is to see my head atop a young woman's half-clothed body.

But I was using this costume only as the basis for a more elaborate one. With my own paints I had added a gorgeous multi-colored necklace of eight strands, a golden belt with the misspelled word "Cleopatera," and a golden cape that fell to the sides of the nubile body. After donning this disguise I pulled on a golden mask that covered the top half of my face.

Then I topped it off by covering my beige hairdo with a huge black, curly wig, on which I had installed a cardboard coronet painted gold.

On the black shoulder-length curls I hung golden tassels originally made for furniture (I remembered seeing those decadent-looking tassels in the movie featuring Elizabeth Taylor).

I added gold-colored ankle bracelets made of heavy paper, and I slipped on a pair of black flip-flops. (Sorry, Nurse Noonan.)

To complete this garish vision, I pinned the small black mandala to the bra section of the painted bathing suit.

I wanted to keep this apparition secret until the last moment, so I used a long black silk opera cape to cover Cleo's body before I walked out the door.

If this doesn't do it, I thought determinedly, nothing will.

TWENTY-FIVE

I was thinking of Helene as I approached the Big Game Room, pushing my flip-flops along awkwardly and pretending to be comfortable in my costume. Helene would probably not attend this party, but because of our regard for her she would be there in spirit.

Then I realized that other costumed people, instead of entering the party room, had lined up outside it. "What's going on here?" I inquired of one of the Beatles.

A woman's voice emanating from the Beatle costume replied, "It appears that members of this group all have short programs for their characters to present, so we are going in one at a time. Except that the first two are together, so they are entering two at once. The rest of us are..."

"Yes, yes, I get it," placing myself at the end of the line. Peering into the room, I saw that residents, many with only partial costumes, were chattering excitedly and milling around at one end, most of them standing, but a few had found seats. Some wore masks and/or headdresses of some kind (I spotted a parrot, an alligator, and The Lone Ranger, not exactly fraternizing), but those of us in the hallway wore complete costumes.

Then I heard Brett Bozeman clap his hands and demand, "Let's begin!" The first two people in line walked into the room, to general acclaim.

From the way they walked, I realized I was watching Bill Hufferman and his girlfriend Katrina. Bill approached the piano wearing the formal hat of the nineteenth and twentieth century called a top hat. It was too large and had to be lodged behind his ears, so it covered his brows. He wore the formal clothes called "tails," although his figure failed to resemble that of knife-thin Fred Astaire, the actor generally associated with this outfit.

For some reason, the jacket of his costume appeared to be sewn to the shirt, so with each step he took, the resulting garment moved up from his waistline, thus revealing more of his ample midsection than we were meant to see.

Unconcerned, Bill placed in front of the piano a sign attached to a signholder. The words read "Fremch Chamtreuse," deliberately misspelled, of course. Bowing, and bulging more at the waist, he lifted his coattails (offering us a better skin view, to screams of appreciation from the audience) and sat down. The "Chamtreuse" moved to the fore. The piano struck up, and we concentrated on the singer.

As she gazed at her audience, we realized we were looking at the world-weary face of Edith Piaf, the singer who often appeared in a sequin-covered evening gown and who tried to convey sadness and pain by singing through her nose. Her sunken cheeks (created with brown makeup) and her thin eyebrows (painted to descend to her cheekbones at the ends), her dark red lipstick, and her curly red wig contributed considerably to her nasal delivery of "La Vie En Rose."

She achieved this delivery by compressing tongue to palate, thus producing a remarkable "NNNNN" sound. Near the end of her song, the result seemed less nasal than she desired, so she placed a clothespin on her nose and finished the song.

Applause for this act was loud and appreciative. I also saw the Lone Ranger dropping his whip and choking on his ginger ale. A sound like "Har! Har! Har!" was apparently emanating from the parrot I'd spied earlier. Edith picked up her sign, and she and her accompanist joined the crowd.

"Next act," called Brett Bozeman.

Out stepped a character we soon identified as the famous Popeye of many years ago. His walk was swaggering, and he displayed muscled forearms created by tan-colored cloth wrappings. Wearing navy jeans, a black sailor's blouse, and a white cap, he marched around smoking (upside-down) a small and ugly black pipe while carrying an open can labeled "Spinush" out of which spilled some grasslike substance. Then he began his redundant and less-than-melodic song:

I'm Popeye the sailor man,
I'm Popeye the sailor man.
I'm strong to the finich
cause I eats me spinach.
I'm Popeye the sailor man.

After singing that authentic but boring ditty, he performed what was evidently meant to be a hornpipe, humming its tune as he danced. His too-small cap hopped up and down, detracting somewhat from the seriousness of the dance. But he could not complete the performance because he pulled a muscle and had to be assisted to a seat.

It was while Popeye was singing — if his presentation could be dignified by the name — that I realized we were watching our friend Lucas in action. Applause was punctuated with remarks, some of them rather sarcastic. "Where's Olive?" someone shouted. "Strong men don't smoke," called someone else. "He's healthy because he eats grass," commented the alligator.

"Let's go!" called Brett Bozeman, beckoning to the next in line.

And out came Judy Garland, carrying a straw basket and wearing a blue pinafore with ruffles, a pleated white blouse, and white sox with black shoes. A large white bow lay limply on the top of her head. She seemed a perky little thing until she started to sing "I'm off to see the wizard" in a man's voice.

Then the howls of laughter drowned her out. She tried to move in a girlish way while singing, but soon the calls of "Boo!" and "Give her the hook!" covered the voice, which by then we had identified as Ed Champion's. "Judy" bowed and moved girlishly into the crowd, and her friends ventured to clap for her, although a few roared.

Brett waved his hand at the lineup, and some people gasped at the next character: one of the Beatles in a black suit without lapels. His long bob culminated in bangs so luxurious that they covered his eyebrows and endangered his vision. He carried some kind of instrument; I think it was a 1930s ukulele.

As he peered out from under those bangs, we realized that his mouth was pulled back in a way to permit a view of a couple of teeth larger than the others. "Ugh!' was a remark from one member of the audience. Another called out, "Which one are you? Ringo?" The answer came in a woman's voice: "Does it matter?"

Then, pretending to play the instrument, the Beatle began singing "It's been a hard day's night," but he mixed up some of the phrases so that one line became "When I get home you are sleeping like a dog." The audience demonstrated loud appreciation for this edited version of the original song, which, after fifty years, we were all tired of hearing. So the Beatle, who was Starr, received a lot of applause.

Then it was my turn.

TWENTY-SIX

I glided into the room, or tried to, despite the slapping sound my flip-flops made on the floor. To begin, I swept aside my dramatic cloak, throwing it onto the piano with a grand gesture, although it fell to the floor instead. Some of the audience responded with "Ooh!" or "Wow!" when they saw the bathing suit that covered small amounts of skin, but when they realized the suit was painted on cloth, they started to laugh. I took this as a good sign and began my act.

I moved sinuously—or in a way I thought could be interpreted as sinuously—turning all the way around so that the audience could see the full Monty. Giggles and shrieks from the audience. Then I began my song, which was really more of a chant, since I can't carry a tune.

I am Cleopatera,
the great Egyptian flatterah.
I could raise a spark
both from Caesar and from Mark.
I caused a war with Rome,
And both those guys went home.

My audience seemed not to care that this rhyme offered a slightly foreshortened version of the past and clapped as if I had just presented a profound history lesson.

To indicate the end of my performance, I bowed, and my headdress started to tip forward. I caught it in time and tore off my mask so that I could see better, discovering with clearer vision that in performing my song I had been addressing the piano. But nobody seemed to mind, and the clapping, punctuated by howls, was loud as I walked toward the crowd, looking for an empty seat.

Before I reached the chair, there was a disturbance in the group. Someone with a square mustache painted on his upper lip, wearing a tattered jacket, baggy pants, and a small derby, came forward.

As I watched him shuffle toward me, I realized that I was looking at Charlie Chaplin as "The Little Tramp," his most famous character. I smiled and clapped, and so did those around me as they turned toward Charlie, who looked as sad and bedraggled as Chaplin had portrayed him in those early movies. We were looking at an excellent costume—and wondering why Charlie had not lined up to perform for us.

Then Charlie spoke softly, in a woman's voice: "May I talk to you?"

"Of course. Cleopatra grants audiences to her subjects."

It was then that I recognized the woman's voice as that of Shelley Pace. And I began to understand.

We sat together in a corner while someone dressed and masked as Clint Eastwood's Dirty Harry character moved forward and put on an impromptu act: "Loretta put sugar in my coffee today. Smith and Wesson and I won't let you get away with this. So, go ahead. Make. My. Day." He raised his thumb and forefinger in a simulated gun and said "Bang!"

This act became so popular that he—I mean, Annabelle—had to repeat it several times, until she inadvertently poked her "gun" finger in Clarence's eye, and Joan went out for wet compresses.

While all this was going on, Shelley said softly to me, "I believe you have something that belongs to me."

I smiled. "Yes. It's beautiful. I think you own more like this." I unpinned it and handed it to her.

She nodded. "I'm ashamed to admit it."

"The Wet Bathing Suit was yours."

"It was. My mistake was in thinking that a man who had found me attractive forty years ago would continue to do so if I — well, you realize what I did. It was stupid. I'm sorry I felt unable to come forward sooner."

"I understand. I'll see that the bathing suit is disposed of. And I'll save your other pin for you."

"You're very kind."

"Where did you get the pins?"

"The Museum of Art in New York — the Metropolitan."

"In the shop?"

"Yes. The museum has a collection of mandalas painted on silk. Some were copied as pins for the museum shop. You should see the originals some time. They might inspire you to create more designs of your own."

"One thing about that bathing suit. You are rather thin for a size 14."

Shelley smiled. "The suit is padded in strategic places."

It felt strange to be sitting next to Charlie Chaplin, talking about pins and bathing suits. Yet somehow I knew that I was not experiencing one of my alternate visions.

In a few minutes Brett Bozeman announced that he and Polly had decided the winner of the best costume: the Fremch Chamtreuse. After that, it was time to visit the bar and continue the party.

TWENTY-SEVEN

Patricia Knightsbridge took only an hour to respond to my phone message informing her that my still life was ready and that I was holding a little reception in my apartment on Saturday afternoon to show it to my friends. I think she wondered why my friends would be as interested as she was, but she said nothing then.

For those who liked my choice of booze, Harvey's Bristol Cream, I furnished two bottles. For others, I'd assembled whiskey, vodka, and wine, along with snacks made of red-pepper hummus on rice crackers. I had uncovered the painting, and it stood on an easel in the middle of my studio.

Those who arrived to examine it were surprised, because at first it seemed to represent the Locksley Glen pool court quite exactly—a standard still life. Gradually, they began to realize that there was more to read in the story it told. One by one they recognized that the chaise longue in the foreground bore something black, something that represented a familiar item.

"I know what's lying there." Katrina was the first one to recognize it. "It's the Wet Bathing Suit!" Not unexpected, as Katrina has a habit of saying the obvious.

"I see something gleaming on the suit," declared Starr. "That little black and white object."

"It's Shelley's mandala pin," Annabelle declared. She turned to me. "What you said to her was very nice. She's your friend for life now."

"I was glad we had a chance to talk about it quietly."

"What's this thing in the corner? A leg?" Bob Avery asked.

"You have a good eye for legs, Bob."

"You mean that's someone running away from the bathing suit?"

"Precisely."

"And I see her tiny footprints on the path!" declared Joan. "How cute!"

Of course, I meant it to be dramatic, not cute, because the viewer was supposed to wonder why the bare-legged woman had left her bathing suit on the chaise longue and was running away from it. I said nothing, however.

Ed Champion figured it out. "She's escaping from that wet bathing suit. It represents a mistake she made. We all make them."

Patricia Knightsbridge seemed impressed with all this analysis, but she didn't know what we were talking about, so she just smiled.

THE END

We hope you enjoyed Dorothy Syemour Mills' second novel of the *Don't Admit You Live in Assited Living* series, *Mystery Two: The Wet Bathing Suit.* Be sure to look into her other two books in the series, *Mystery One: The Kiss,* and her concluding story, the *Third Mystery: The Phone Call.*

CPSIA information can be obtained
at www.ICGtesting.com
Printed in the USA
FFOW05n1447261217

9 781604 521313